WESTMINSTER PUBLIC LIBRARY
3 3020 01146 3196

D0961746

Love in the Big City

Sang Young Park

Love in the Big City

a novel

Translated from the Korean by Anton Hur

Grove Press
New York

Originally published in Korea in 2019 as *Daedosiui Sarangbeop* by Changbi Publishers.

Simultaneously published in the United Kingdom by Tilted Axis Press.

Published simultaneously in Canada
Printed in the United States of America

First Grove Atlantic hardcover edition: November 2021

This book is published with the support of the Literature Translation Institute of Korea (LTI Korea).

Library of Congress Cataloging-in-Publication data is available for this title.

ISBN 978-0-8021-5878-9
eISBN 978-0-8021-5879-6

Grove Press
an imprint of Grove Atlantic
154 West 14th Street
New York, NY 10011

Distributed by Publishers Group West

groveatlantic.com

21 22 23 24 10 9 8 7 6 5 4 3 2 1

Love in the Big City

PART ONE

Jaehee

1.

I took the elevator to the third floor of the hotel and went into the Emerald Hall. Had she said the guest list was four hundred people? It looked like a lot more than that. I sat down in my designated seat and looked around the table: my cohort of French majors, all of us aging at different speeds. How many of them were there? I guess this was the reward for Jaehee saying yes to every postgraduation bender and homecoming-day event. Moments like these made Jaehee's social life seem to border on the grotesque. I was forced to acknowledge acquaintances I hadn't talked to in five, even ten years. "Congratulations! I hear you're a writer now." "You should get in touch more often." "Hey, there was a rumor that you'd died, but here you are!" "Where can I find your stories? I tried searching for them on the Internet." "Wow, writing must be tough on you. Look at how much weight you've gained." "Do you still drink as much as you used to?"

My book is about to come out, I don't drink as much as I used to, you guys are just as old and fat as I am, and your questions are about to drive me to old drinking habits—these answers were all on the tip of my tongue, but I swallowed them, upholding the dignity of an educated contributor to society in his thirties and laughing off their snideness. I'd been ready to swear to anyone who read my stories that everything I wrote was made up—how silly of me to have prepared an answer for a question that would never be asked. An excess of self-awareness was a disease in itself.

—Please take your seats, the ceremony is about to begin.

The emcee was a close friend of Jaehee's husband-in-progress. This friend had a sharp chin and greasy skin, not my type at all, and on top of his thick Gyeongsang Province accent, it was all too clear that this country boy wasn't great at moving things along. And he was a television reporter somehow? I'd have been a much better choice. Who cared about these stupid traditions about whose-best-friend-does-what anymore? The green monster of jealousy was rearing its head.

Next to the platform was a large screen that was flashing photos of Jaehee and her groom. I took another sip of red wine as the low-resolution phone-camera photos flicked by. Cheolgu—who sat next to me and had apparently gotten a job at the Industrial Bank recently—poked me in the ribs.

—Be honest with me. You and Jaehee. Were the rumors true?

The rumors were true, but, dear Cheolgu, what you're implying seems a little rich coming from the guy who asked Jaehee out only to be viciously snubbed.

◊

The summer we turned twenty, Jaehee and I became best friends.

I had a funny drinking rule back then—I would do anything I was told by whoever bought me a drink—and so on that fateful day, there I was again with a man of an uncertain age in the Hamilton Hotel parking lot, sucking face. He had bought me about six shots of tequila at some basement club. The moon and streetlamps and neon signs of the whole world seemed to be shining their lights just for me, and I could still hear the strains of a Kylie Minogue remix in my ear. It wasn't important who the guy was. The only thing that mattered was that I existed with someone, there in those dark streets of the city, and that was why I was wrestling tongues with a stranger. Just when I thought the heat of the whole world was about to overflow, just for me, I felt a hard slap on my back. In the midst of my complete drunkenness I thought, *A hate crime!* And in full drama-queen mode, I detached my lips from his and turned around, ready for a fistfight—but there stood Jaehee. As always, she was holding a lipstick-smudged Marlboro Red in one hand, and the sight of her instantly sobered me up. Jaehee could barely catch her breath as she laughed at how shocked I was to see her. Then she said, in her typically brash voice:

—Just eat him, why don't you?

Before I knew what was happening, I'd burst out laughing at her joke, and at some point I realized the man I was kissing had disappeared, and I can't even recall his face now. But I do remember more or less what Jaehee and I talked about in the parking lot.

—You'll keep it a secret around campus, right?

—Of course. I'm a broke bitch, but I'm loyal.

—Weren't you surprised? Me with a man.

—Not at all.

—Since when did you know?

—Since the moment I laid eyes on you.

The usual cliché.

Up until then I didn't know Jaehee very well; she was just a girl who wore short-shorts and was always first to run out of class, desperate for a cigarette. Actually, she was pretty close to having the worst reputation in the department.

Even if I did end up an outsider among the French majors at our college, I hadn't been like that from the beginning, when I was still invited to parties by our male upperclassmen sunbaes just because I happened to be a taller-than-average male. These gatherings always took the same course, all the guys going to the pool hall or PC rooms first, then to a restaurant specializing in MSG cuisine to make the soju flow, then picking one of the less messy sunbaes' rooms to drink more and talk about girls until we collapsed, snoring. Standard-issue nineteen- and twenty-year-olds talking about what a big deal they were and what great sex they were having, how well they satisfied their women, which of the French department girls were easy. And Jaehee was someone they kept returning to. Listening to their stories that were obviously at least half fiction, and fed up with wondering why I had to put up with this shit even in college, I came to a point where I drunk-shouted, "Fucking stop it with the bullshit, you all have faces like *rat dicks*," and flipped the table, after which I was never invited to hang out again.

As is the nature of any group, a member who had fled the fold was inevitably fated to remain as gossip fodder thereafter. Tired of their exhaustive critiques of the female frosh, they tossed me into the meat grinder instead, saying I seemed gay and was hanging out in Itaewon doing God knows what, spreading the kind of rumors only a bunch of innocent nineteen-year-olds would care about, half of which were true. (Truth always surpasses fiction.) Barely a semester had gone by when almost the entire department knew who I was, and I'd heard the rumors myself, making me the butt of everyone's jokes. *I guess I'll never make friends in this department, not that they can drink to save their lives, and they're boring as hell.* As I was consoling myself with such self-justifications, Jaehee veered into my life.

After my defense of her sort of outed me, the two of us developed a relationship that consisted in the first place of talking trash about boys, as neither of us had previously had anyone with whom to share such thoughts, making us both desperate for a sounding board.

Jaehee and I had very little sense of chastity, or none at all, to be honest, and we were apparently known for it in our respective spheres. Jaehee was five foot six and 112 pounds, while I was five ten and 172 pounds, both a bit taller than average but neither particularly attractive nor a complete lost cause, just enough not to embarrass any partner. (Note that when I won a New Writers Award for fiction, the judges' comments were united in their praise of my "objective self-judgment"). The world was just not ready for the boundless energy of poor, promiscuous twenty-year-olds. We met whatever men we wanted without putting much effort into it, drank ourselves torpid, and in the morning met in each other's rooms to apply cosmetic masks to our swollen faces and exchange tidbits about the men we had been with the night before.

—He works at a company that makes hiking gear. Small dick but good foreplay, I think worth fifty points?

—He says he went to Yonsei University, studying statistics, but I think that's a lie. His face was a blank space, and I kept wanting to laugh because whenever he said something, it was obvious his head was just as empty.

—He tried to take a video while we were in bed, so I threw his phone across the room. He said he wasn't going to share it with anyone, like I'd ever believe that bullshit.

And after we made fun of the men from the previous night, our eyes would begin to close and we'd fall asleep side by side, with dried-up masks on our faces. Being an early riser, I would get up first and let Jaehee rest longer, with the quilt pulled all the way up over her head, as I boiled instant pollack stew or ramen, and when it was ready Jaehee would finally get up at the smell and eat the breakfast with sides of soured kimchi and cold rice. At some point, Jaehee's room had an extra set of my hair wax and a Gillette razor, while my room had a double of Jaehee's eyebrow pencil and MAC powder compact. Jaehee didn't know this, but when I was alone, I used her liner to fill in the gaps in my eyebrows and helped myself to her compact to half-heartedly apply a puff or two of concealer on my cheeks and forehead. Which made me wonder if Jaehee used my razor on her legs or armpits without telling me.

Jaehee stopped talking to her mother and father the spring she turned twenty. Neither of us had been on good terms with our parents, but that didn't mean they were especially evil or anything more than typical middle-class conservatives. Like most people's parents, they constantly nagged their children about propriety and how one should behave, but in their own private lives joyfully indulged in affairs, excess religion, the stock market, or pyramid schemes. I had a real parasitic streak in that as much as I hated my parents, I felt completely entitled to every coin they gave me (was that why my demeanor grew mischievous?)

when I was receiving hundreds of thousands of won in monthly allowance. Jaehee, however, cut off contact with her parents after their blowout and refused any form of financial support thereafter. She really did have the heart of a lioness.

She got her first-ever job working at a café called Destiné. She picked it not because it had a large sign with a French name but because it was one of the few places in her neighborhood where smoking was allowed. The sight of her puffing away as she handled the espresso machines was a vision of oblivious nineteen-year-old cuteness. Whenever I had some man in my life, I'd bring him to Destiné for Jaehee to give him the once-over, and every time, she would tell me that the men I liked were always horny with classic asshole personalities. Thinking back, she was right.

By day, Jaehee worked as a barista, while by night she was a private tutor, and then after that she drank until dawn like it was a third job. But she never missed a class, and her grades were OK, and while she did better than average at anything she put her mind to, this talent didn't extend to her ability to choose men who weren't a total mess, or to dump said men when the time was right. Which was why I often ended up getting rid of her men via text messages. I, on the other hand, was very practiced in that skill—at least vicariously—because of all the lines I'd heard from men who refused to see me again, easy enough to regurgitate at a moment's notice. I used to think of myself as the doormat of a naengmyeon restaurant: all you had to do was wipe your feet on it and be on your way ("objective self-judgment"!).

Around the time the Brown Eyed Girls' "Abracadabra" had conquered the Korean peninsula, I received a summons for national service. Because I knew of someone who during his service had received a letter from his boyfriend that began with "My loving hyung" and was outed for it, resulting in untold torture throughout his time in the army, I instructed K, the guy I was going out with, to write to me under Jaehee's name. She was a handy smokescreen in times like this. I asked not only K but the real Jaehee to write me funny crap while I was in there, but knowing how lazy she was about that kind of thing, I didn't expect much from her.

Yet during the second week of boot camp, when the letters began arriving, I felt my heart rise up to my throat. Unlike K, who had acted like he'd have given me his liver or spleen if I had asked for it but in two weeks had written me only a single letter (and not even a whole page at that), Jaehee had written twelve. At first it was just chitchat about her boring day ("I was drinking at Squid Ocean and accidentally tipped over the table") or cursing out the people in our department ("that fucking nut Cheolgu asked me to sleep with him when I know for a fact he's talking shit about me behind my back, he's as disgusting as his face"), but as the days wore on, she wrote more about the times we had together and how much she missed me. In her latest missive she even said, "There's something to be said about realizing how precious something is once you've lost it. Like with you"—God knows where she got that from—and even though I knew she'd written it drunk, I was almost moved to tears. That made me take up a sheet of military-issue stationery and begin my response to her with "To my dear, ugly Jaehee," trying hard to keep the letters straight.

Around the time I left boot camp and was assigned to my regiment, I heard news that Jaehee had reconnected with her parents and, thanks to them, was being sent to Australia as an exchange student. She also informed me that K seemed suspicious, and suggested I interrogate him when I had the chance. (It didn't take long for her instincts to be proven correct.) Jaehee served as my loyal girlfriend throughout my six months of military service, up until the incident that earned me a medical discharge.

By the time I was banished back to civilian society—and back to my mother's house—Jaehee was already in Australia. Which meant I had to spend about half a year without her until she returned. Not really having anything I wanted to do or anyone else I wanted to see, I mostly lay in bed in my room and ate and slept. My umma was a parent who found such an attitude most contemptible, and her constant nagging eventually drove me to find my own place, a tiny goshitel unit near campus where I could finally be alone.

◊

The new year arrived, and I was there to greet Jaehee when she landed at Incheon International Airport. She saw me standing at the gate and dropped her wheelie suitcase, running to embrace me. The scent of cigarettes in her hair truly brought home that we were finally back together.

Almost the moment Jaehee got back to Korea, she found herself a 350-square-foot studio apartment, registered at an English hagwon, and studied hard to get her TOEIC score up. She also declared a minor in economics, joined a marketing club, and began to look like every other undergraduate preparing themselves for the job market. This new Jaehee felt alien to me, but when I saw her going out to drink seven days a week again, I was reassured that she was the Jaehee of old after all.

Not long after she moved into her new place, Jaehee started noticing something unnerving. Every night at ten, some man would come to her building and stare up at her window.

—Well, jeonse rentals are pretty rare now, maybe he's a realtor?

Despite my glib reply, I was a little bothered by the whole thing. Once, she said she was in her underwear, drying her hair, when their eyes happened to meet. Jaehee added that the ceilings were low and she was only on the second floor, so he could easily climb into her apartment using the balcony. If she was so worried, why didn't she let me stay over for a couple of nights, given that despite everything I was still a man? Jaehee replied she wasn't that worried, but it *was* pretty boring at night and she wouldn't mind the company.

Like a schoolboy going on a class trip, I packed underwear and a tank top and shorts for clothes to sleep in and headed to Jaehee's apartment. We made Japanese curry and watched an idiotic TV show, on which panelists gave advice about the love lives of celebrities, while we simultaneously criticized everything the panelists were saying. I lay in bed and fiddled around with my phone while Jaehee took a shower. She had come out toweling her hair when I glimpsed a shadow behind the curtain. I was looking at it, my brain as blank as a sheet, when Jaehee strode to the window and whipped back the curtain. A man as skinny as a twig was crouched next to the air conditioner's outdoor fan unit. *Oh wow, it's true,* I had just barely managed to think, before Jaehee, in a series of tightly executed moves, slid open the door to the balcony and kicked the dumbstruck man in the face. He fell over backwards. He moaned and raised his head, blood spurting from his nose and mouth. Jaehee had been brought up in a neighborhood where they took education seriously, which meant she had taken piano and tae kwon do lessons since kindergarten, achieving dan 2 in the second grade; such was the power of early learning. I held on to the man, who was barely conscious at that point, and shouted at Jaehee to call both 112 (the police) and 119 (the medics). It was hard not to laugh.

Four days later, I put all of my things into a bag and moved into Jaehee's apartment.

We didn't have a contract or anything. I agreed to pay her 300,000 won in rent and half the utilities. A lot of my things were already in her house anyway, 350 square feet was more than enough space for two to live comfortably, and neither of us had ever had a real relationship by the time we reached our mid-twenties, which meant the closest person we had at the time was each other.

Jaehee was good at making sweet perilla-leaf soy sauce preserves, and I had my special recipe for spicy vongole pasta. I was an expert at washing dishes spotlessly, and Jaehee's courageous soul allowed her to swipe the shower drain clean of clogged hair. After seeing me snacking on frozen blueberries, she always stocked the freezer with bulk-size bags of frozen American blueberries.

In return, I bought her favorite cigarettes, Marlboro Reds, and stacked them next to the blueberries in the freezer. Jaehee said she loved how cool her lips felt whenever she smoked the first cigarette from a new pack.

2.

When Jaehee said she was getting married, the first thing I said was, "Are you pregnant?" Jaehee commented that everyone had reacted that exact same way, without a single exception, and cackled. Surprisingly, she wasn't, nor had she gone anywhere near getting pregnant. Things had just turned out that way—that was the way she put it. And her putting it so made me think it was serious this time.

Jaehee? Getting married?

I couldn't quite believe it. It was more likely that I would take a bride than she a groom. Jaehee just seemed too far removed from the idea of stability and settling down.

◊

When we reached our mid-twenties, Jaehee drank and went out with multiple men as if it were an Olympic sport and she were competing for gold. Since I hated losing, and since I was into booze and men to begin with, I also got drunk and slept with a new man every night. And every morning, I realized anew that the world was filled with lonely people as I walked out of the motel cluster in the Jongno district with my hair in disarray. Some of the men I met wanted more than just drinking followed by a one-night stand. No matter how many times I refused, they kept going on about wanting to date me and threatening to come see me at my apartment, at which point I would fend them off by saying I had a roommate.

—A roommate?

After discussing how we would tell a partner about each other, Jaehee and I decided that the male version of her would be Jaeho, a supposed cohort in the department, and I would be the lovely Jieun, a friend from back home. In each other's worlds we lived as Jaeho and Jieun, perfect excuses for keeping men at bay.

For example, Jaehee might receive a text from her (temporary) boyfriend:

Hey Jaehee, why did you turn your phone off last night? And not look at your texts?

Ugh. Jieun got sick last night. I was in the ER with her all night! ("Jieun" had been perfectly fine and was snoring away at home while Jaehee was drinking five bottles of soju with guys from school.)

Hyung, are you free this weekend?

Sorry. Jaeho and I are going to the Han River for some beer. ("Jaeho" was probably busy meeting up to have sex with men, and I was probably going to fuck someone else before dumping you.)

That kind of thing.

Jaehee's fifth or sixth man had dropped out of a technical school where he'd been learning about fixing boilers and was now going from club to nameless club, allegedly a DJ. My eighth or ninth boyfriend had also been a "DJ" in Itaewon. There were so many DJs in Seoul that I wondered if there ought to be some regulating association that handed out licenses in order to ensure quality spins. But the one I met had a big dick, lots of tattoos, put on good music when we had sex, and was just the right amount of stupid, which allowed us to shape up into a pretty normal couple for a little bit. But two months in he said he loved me but couldn't bring himself to love me when I was drunk (when I'd sing on the street and kiss him and curse and make a scene before inevitably collapsing into tears at the end) and therefore couldn't see me anymore, which left me with a very rational grudge against all DJs. Jaehee, who had no inkling of my complex feelings, spoke about her new boyfriend with a face filled with joy and animation.

—His hair is so long he has it in two braids. He looks just like a doll. It's hilarious when we have sex.

She showed me a photo in which he didn't look at all hilarious, with his cruel gaze that made me think he'd turn into an asshole on a dime. He kept insisting Jaehee bring Jieun (aka me) to the club because he wanted to see my face, but Jaehee would always bluntly refuse.

—She's really, really shy.

Really, really shy Jieun was actually sneaking a look as she sat down at a table next to Jaehee and her boyfriend, eavesdropping on them and discreetly glancing at the man to size him up. His manner of speech, facial expressions, everything about him gave me a bad feeling.

—Jaehee, why do you like that guy?

—I don't know, because he treats me well?

—You're only giving him the time of day because his dick is big, right?

Jaehee's face looked like Moses's gazing at the burning bush as she asked me how I knew that, and I replied out of jealous spite:

—It's my God-given talent.

Marveling, Jaehee confessed to me that I was right, the only thing he had going for him was the size of his genitals, to which I spake unto her that he was surely of lowly consequence and that she must leave him and return to the light, whereupon she vowed to offer up any man she met thenceforth to me for inspection, grasping my hand and gazing at me like a true believer. Nodding sagely, I embraced Jaehee's poor soul.

And, unfortunately, my God-given talent was proven once again.

I had come home from classes one day to find Jaehee's face as white as a sheet. In her hand was a home pregnancy test. Not even putting down my bag, I looked right at the two lines on the small window. My jaw dropped.

—Jesus, can't you limit yourself to doing one thing at a time?

—I'm fucked, aren't I?

—What do you mean, "fucked"? Grab your bag, we're going to the clinic.

—Sure, that's all we need to do, but there's a problem.

—What.

—I'm utterly broke. Penniless.

—You didn't make this baby on your own, we'll shake the boy down.

—That's the real problem.

—What's the real problem? Just spit it out.

—I don't know which boy I'm supposed to shake down.

According to the story that followed, the idiot DJ she was head over heels with was all right at sex but had a terrible personality and was the worst ever when drunk. Worse, he was stupid enough to believe that his personality was proof of an artistic soul, which made Jaehee more determined than ever to finally dump him. She had just been introduced by a coworker at the café to an art student who was our age, and she'd found out only later on that he had long since dropped out of art school and was working as a tattoo artist. The day Jaehee went on her first blind date with him, I just happened to be spending the night elsewhere; she had no choice (?) but to bring him into our apartment and have wild sex with him. But without a condom. It's human nature to find the first time difficult and every subsequent time easier, meaning Jaehee had unprotected sex a few times more. With both men.

—The DJ is better at sex and the tattoo guy is better looking, which gave me a lot to think about.

In this, the Great Information Age, you might imagine she would've processed her thoughts a lot faster, like a normal person, but Jaehee was locked in an unsolvable dilemma as she ping-ponged between the two men for three months. I said to her that if she had this dilemma twice more, she'd end up with enough children for an orphanage, a quip she ignored. She showed me a photo on her phone. The tattoo artist's face, she said. The man she showed me had shorter hair than the DJ but was otherwise surprisingly similar, and as skinny as a dried-up anchovy you wouldn't even try to boil for broth.

—He looks the same as the other guy. I bet you can just have the baby and claim either man is the father?

Jaehee seemed too down to even laugh at my joke. Most uncharacteristically, she began to mumble things like "I should've drunk less . . . I can't even afford food . . . I can't ask my umma for the money, what do I do?" Which was so annoying to me that I just said:

—Forget them. I'll give you the money.

—Hey . . . That's too much.

—I'm not just giving it to you for free. I expect it back, with interest. But get it done quickly for now, all right?

—Really? Are you serious? You're the best. Thank you.

Jaehee changed from the jeans she was wearing to a dress with an elastic waist, and then began to put on makeup. Her lipstick was a color I hadn't seen before, and when I asked when she'd gotten it, she popped her lips a few times at her reflection and said she'd bought it at a Hyundai department store a few days ago. Before I could stop myself, I cried:

—How could you be putting on Dior lipstick at a time like this?

As if I had the right to scold, like I'd ever done anything for her in my life. She was putting on her sneakers like slippers, not bothering to slip her heels into them. I said to the back of her head:

—You're the one getting surgery, so why do I feel nervous?

—There's nothing to it. Think of it as getting a pimple popped.

—Not the same thing.

I said it with a growl but felt a little relieved. All right, if she herself was fine with it, no need for me to get overdramatic. Her impervious (close to insensitive) personality that normally irritated me was a source of huge relief now.

We headed to a nearby gynecologist. She said the doctor there was rude and the place a dump, but she began going there when they offered a 40 percent discount on HPV vaccines. Whether the specialist even did abortions was a separate issue. "Shouldn't you have researched that on the Internet beforehand," I asked, but there was no way Jaehee would spend even a microsecond thinking about that kind of thing. She said if they didn't do abortions, we'd go somewhere else. No one was better than her at bumbling through life's important decisions.

The clinic truly was a dump. We were the only people there, which got Jaehee a meeting with the doctor as soon as she registered. I sat to wait on a sofa so old that it had permanent butt depressions in its seats. On the walls were posters of all kinds of viruses, the diseases they caused, and the miraculous medicines that cured them, as well as a little blackboard advertising summer deals on laser hair removal, Botox, and fillers. I read all of them while waiting for Jaehee, musing over how much it would cost to make my stupid face more tolerable. It was taking longer than I thought for her to get an appointment. The young nurse sitting at the reception desk yawned. They weren't going to do the procedure today, were they? What was taking so long . . . ?

Unwrapping a couple of the plum-favored candies on the table and popping them in my mouth, I thought about the urology clinic I'd gone to a few months back. It had a similar vibe.

At first, my urethra had tingled a bit when I peed, but after a while it felt as uncomfortable as if someone were squeezing it, prompting me to get it checked. And since I was going to the clinic near the university subway station, I figured I should take the engineering student I was seeing with me. I felt it was right because we'd done it a few times at that point. An innocent mistake on my part.

After peeing into a cup and getting that analyzed, I learned the results weren't some dramatic STD, just my urethra infected by germs, and inflammation resulting from it. "I didn't know you could get infected in there," I mumbled to myself, and the doctor, with a concerned expression, delivered an unsolicited lecture about how a woman's genitals featured many kinds of bacteria and in some cases the urethra would get infected. Feeling weirdly guilty, I closed the consultation room door behind me, face red. Slightly embarrassed, I went into the injection room and was lying there with my trousers halfway down when I heard across the silence two male nurses talking to each other behind a partition.

—Did you see those two? I'm right, aren't I?

—Yeah. Faggots.

—Fuck, so disgusting.

Before I could stop myself, I burst out laughing. The engineering student I'd come with said there was no trace of an infection in his sample. I joked about what I'd heard in the injection room, but the engineering student immediately flew into a rage and demanded to see the two assholes who had said such bullshit. Watching his reaction, I finally realized this was something I should've been angry about from the beginning, and that I had a tendency to laugh loudly in situations where I should be angry. The shot I received that day was painful, and I went out with the engineering student a few more times until it became boring and I stopped returning his messages.

In the midst of reminiscing about my great past loves, I suddenly heard Jaehee screaming inside the consultation room. The nurse who had followed her in opened the door and said to me, with an apologetic expression, "I think you should come in here." Inside, neither doctor nor patient looked like they had the wherewithal to pay me any attention. The middle-aged doctor, with an angry face, was waving a small ultrasound printout right under Jaehee's nose.

—This is all because of the way you live your life. Understand?

—Fuck this, I can't take it anymore.

Just when the doctor was about to say something else, Jaehee grabbed her bag and stood up. And that's not all she grabbed; she also picked up the 3D model of the uterus on the desk. I had just enough time to think of the word *What?* before Jaehee ran out of the consultation room with it. The doctor got up and shouted:

—Hey! Put that back!

Jaehee was gone like the wind, and there was no point in following her. She had, after all, been a champion sprinter up until middle school.

I was left to pay the consultation fee: 48,900 won. Feeling sorry about the whole thing, I said to the nurse:

—I'll get the model uterus back to you right away. She has no endurance, she won't have gone far.

The nurse answered me with a long sigh.

Sure enough, Jaehee was only a few steps outside the building, hugging the model womb as she leaned on a utility pole. As soon as she saw me, she waved an arm in the air, asking for a light. I took out a lighter from my pocket and held it out to the Marlboro Red in her mouth. Jaehee stared at the model uterus and said:

—It's so fucking old.

—He must've bought it on graduation day. It says he entered SNU medical school in 1988.

—How did you find *that* out?

—I was so bored I read his doctor's license on the wall.

—I've made a decision. Never deal with shits from Seoul National University.

—Fuck SNU for a minute, why did you have to do that? If he wasn't going to do the procedure, you should've just left.

—I wouldn't have screamed at him like that for no reason. He's a psychopath. Listen to this.

As soon as she mentioned she was pregnant, the doctor had immediately made her lie down on the examining bed and administered an ultrasound. The results showed that the fetus (which is what he called the clump of cells) was about eight weeks along.

—He demanded that the father come in and see it, and I told him that you weren't the father and that in fact I had no idea who the father was.

—Would it have killed you to lie? Just make shit up!

—You know I cannot tell a lie.

Which was a lie in itself—the truth was quite the opposite—she just couldn't ever tell a lie when she really needed to. The doctor had gone on a rant about prophylactics and the need for chaste living for over twenty minutes. He flipped through her chart and said her recurring bouts of bladder inflammations could be from promiscuous sexual intercourse and began to berate her about her moral looseness and wild drinking habits. Jaehee, noticing the cross hanging on the wall, had suppressed her anger and replied:

—You know, it's thanks to sluts like me that you can make a living.

—I'm only saying this because you feel like a daughter to me. What are you going to do later on if you're so immoral? Do you know what the worst thing for a woman's body is? Promiscuity and unsafe sex. Don't you understand?

—Actually, pregnancy and birth are the worst things for a woman's body.

—What are you saying?

—I read it on the Internet. A fetus is basically a foreign object lodged inside a woman. And there's nothing worse than pregnancy and giving birth for the body. So just give me the abortion.

—Who says that?! Who?!

The doctor, in a loud and angry voice, lectured her for about another three minutes on the baseness of the Internet and the ignorance of the masses that refused to trust educated people before pulling out the ultrasound scan and waving it at her.

—There's a life already growing inside of you. Why can't you understand that your body is a sacred temple?

—Enough with the sacred bullshit, doctor, just tell me if you'll do the surgery.

The doctor then went on another rant about the importance of (her long-gone) virginity, which was the final straw for Jaehee, who burst out screaming.

Heaving from anger as she recounted all this to me, she said:

—It's smaller than a peanut. How could it be a person?

—OK, I get that. I get all of that, but maybe stealing their uterus model is not in your best interest? It's important to them.

—That's why I stole it.

—You have a point, it's very "you" of you.

I giggled as I smoked a cigarette with her. Soon, I could see the gynecologist's nurse walking up to us. Still as expressionless as she'd been when she was sitting in the reception area, the nurse held out her hand to Jaehee.

—Miss Jaehee. Please give that to me.

—Oh, unni, I'm really sorry about all of that, but he truly was an asshole.

—Yes, I know. He's a decrepit bastard who drives people up the wall, but you're only making things harder for me.

Jaehee rubbed out her cigarette on the pavement.

—All right. But I'm only giving this back for your sake.

As if she had any other choice. The nurse took the model offered to her.

—There's a clinic near Sungshin Women's University. They do abortions, and the service is much better. That's where I go.

—Thank you so much, unni!

Jaehee suddenly embraced the nurse and said she would buy her a drink after it was all over and got her number and everything. *What the hell,* I thought, *does she think drinking money just falls from the sky?*

But you had to admit Jaehee was nothing if not personable.

And so we arrived at the gynecologist near Sungshin Women's University, where I felt cowed by the large pink sign in front of the building. Jaehee saw my reaction and remarked:

—Don't you feel like we're the Fellowship of the Abortion?

I forced a laugh, and we walked arm in arm into the clinic.

The place was like a franchise coffeeshop, spacious, clean, and with mechanically polite staff. Despite the fact that it was midafternoon, there were many patients in the waiting room. (Obviously) I was the only man there. To make it look like I was totally at ease, I sat down on a sofa and opened up an issue of *Cosmopolitan*. It was filled with articles about Healthy and Beautiful Sex, the Different Orgasms of Different Genders, and other subjects that felt totally abstract to me. I was wondering how I could stop nervously biting my nails when Jaehee came back out. She had a bright smile as she whispered:

—They'll do it.

Four days later, she underwent the procedure. I paid for it in three installments: a little less than 700,000 won total. She took a taxi home afterwards. As soon as she got back, she very uncharacteristically went straight to bed, so I decided to make her seaweed soup. Never having cooked it from scratch, I misjudged how much of the dried seaweed I needed and ended up hydrating what looked like a kelp farm in the sink. I grabbed a handful like a wig and waved it over the sink shouting, "Look at this, aren't I the biggest idiot in the world?" But Jaehee didn't so much as turn her head my way. Any other time, she would've cackled along. I said to her back:

—Does it hurt a lot?

—Do you really want to know?

—Nope. This'll be ready soon.

The first seaweed soup I'd made in my life ended in total failure. I didn't cook the meat in the sesame seed oil at the right temperature, which gave it a bitter taste, and all the seasoning salt in the world couldn't take away the blandness of the broth. Jaehee took about three spoonfuls and went back to bed. She moaned and sighed for a bit and then said:

—Cigarette.

—No way! Even double-eyelid surgery makes you rest for four days after.

—Cigarette!

I got her a new pack from the freezer. Jaehee put the yellow filter of the Marlboro Red in her mouth and took a delicious draw.

—Goddamn. I guess I'll live.

Two weeks later, Jaehee returned to the world of functional alcoholism.

◊

One night, we were woken up from our usual drunken stupor by someone's shouting:

—Come out, you fucking bastard!

. . . along with other vociferous invitations of that nature. I covered my head with my blanket. *Fucking asshole, why can't these idiots just go home if they can't hold their alcohol?* But as I tried to fall asleep again, I suddenly had a feeling that the name he was shouting seemed vaguely familiar. It even, kind of, sounded like *my* name. Jaehee also got up, rubbing her eyes, and said:

—I think it's for you. Better get down there.

Opening the window, I saw the engineering student I'd gone to the urologist with standing there in the street. He wasn't much of a drinker to begin with but there he was, dead drunk, and screaming things like "You gay bastard," "You homo," "You faggot"—the works. *Jesus, the things I live to see,* I thought as I dragged my slippered feet downstairs, whereupon the bastard slapped me in the face as soon as I got close enough. Something about me trampling on the sincerity of his love and how I needed to pay the price? He screamed about how he was going to tell my family I was a homosexual and a rag so spoiled I could never be washed clean. *What the fuck is this bullshit about my family?* I thought, then realized I'd fended him off a few times from visiting me at home by claiming I lived with my family. Jaehee came down in her pajamas and mumbled, "Is this shit over yet?" Ignoring the neck-grabbing going on in front of her, she started to smoke. The engineering student pushed me off, went up to Jaehee and said, "Nunim, listen to what your younger brother did to me," and then went on about how many men I went around having sex with and the sex positions I liked and how I had love handles but no ass, to which Jaehee's lack of response prompted him to grab my neck again and scream, "You're going to get sick and you're going to fucking die," over and over like a bad rap song. I yawned and replied:

—You should be a contestant on *Show Me the Money*.

He screamed a bit more and collapsed to the ground in tears.

—Loving someone is not a crime!

—No, loving someone isn't a crime, but you doing this right now sure is, a fairly big one in fact . . . All I did was sleep with you a few times before dumping you . . . I think you may be overreacting just a little bit . . .

As I consoled him, Jaehee kept bursting out with tiny-fart laughs before helping him up to his feet again.

—Hey. Let's go for a drink.

And before I could stop them, they went off arm in arm, leaving me behind. When I tried to follow, she waved me off and told me I should go home.

She came back in a little less than an hour and said everything was taken care of.

—You're a pro. How did you manage to calm him down?

—It was nothing. I pretended to listen to him and waited until he was well and truly drunk. Then put him in a cab.

"Look at this," she added, showing me her phone; she'd taken photos of his student ID and driver's license. His address was in Gaepo-dong, near Gangnam. Another detail caught my eye.

—Damn. He lied to me about his age.

The ID said he was also part of the entering class of '06.

—If he comes back here, we can pay him a return visit in Gaepo-dong.

I hugged Jaehee tight. My devil, my savior, my Jaehee.

* * *

In those days, we learned a little bit about what it was like to live as other people. Jaehee learned that living as a gay was sometimes truly shitty, and I learned that living as a woman wasn't much better. And our conversations always ended with the same question:

—Why were we born this way?

—Who knows?

◊

Throughout this drama, a rumor went around our department about how while we were living together, Jaehee had gotten pregnant and had an abortion. All technically true, which made Jaehee and me marvel at the omniscient wonders of collective intelligence. We were all seniors now anyway, too busy looking for a way to make a living, and such rumors hardly affected the author or the subject of the rumor.

Jaehee overcame her characteristic lack of common sense and maintained good grades while reducing the number of times she got drunk in a week from eight to three, and thus returned to the land of the living. I sat in French literature classes nodding off to geriatric professors blabbering on about love, looked every night for someone to have sex with, and if that didn't work out, sat at home waiting for Jaehee like one of Jeju Island's petrified-rock fishermen's wives of myth, pouring myself a bowl of frozen blueberries. If I ate them with my fingers, my fingers turned purple. For some reason, I found this hilarious.

In the first semester of her senior year, Jaehee defied her job-market handicap of being a female humanities major and scored a job at a large electronics company. During the month she left home to spend at the company training center, I was so bored I almost died. Without Jaehee, there was no one to drink with, have stupid conversations with, or just kill time with. The nights became too long, which got me doing what was so unlike me: poring over the list of men I'd dumped. The engineering student had just got a job at an automobile company and had bought a Kia K3 and (this part is important) wanted any excuse whatsoever to take it out for a drive on the weekends, which suited me fine as well. I hadn't been trying to get back together with him after the whole shouting-from-the-street fiasco, but riding around in that K3 to N Tower and Sanjeong Lake made it seem like we were doing something that resembled coupledom. We'd already had sex enough times for my body to feel like his and his mine, really nothing new there, but we both had low self-esteem, regularly felt suicidal compulsions, were bullied as kids, and pretentiously enjoyed arty films and books while hating basic crap like Haruki Murakami, Hong Sangsoo, French literature, and Audis, all of which made us end up thinking we were something special as a pair.

Jaehee was also not one to waste time, and she managed to find a boyfriend in her corporate cohort who was three years older than her. I thought she would play around with him for a while and dump him, but I realized she was serious about him when, around the three-month mark, she officially invited me to have dinner with them.

—Since it would be weird if you were a third wheel at the dinner, bring your boyfriend.

—He's not my boyfriend.

—Fine. The K3 guy.

—No. That's even weirder. What am I going to introduce him to your boyfriend as?

—Would you quit snapping back at me for a second and just come? It'll be my treat.

—What's the treat?

The first part of the evening was at a fancy Korean restaurant in Hannam-dong. Jaehee's boyfriend was told that we were friends who had met at a board game club. Her boyfriend was different from the previous ones. He did not style himself an artist or regularly slap on a bunch of new tattoos (that he would only be embarrassed about in a year), nor did he have a cunning look in his eye, nor, according to my sixth sense, did he seem to have a big dick. But he had a kind of stability that Jaehee and I didn't have, a fundamental optimism toward life. When I heard he had graduated from Seoul National University Engineering and was working as a researcher in semiconductors, my thumbs tapped out a text to Jaehee from under the table.

I thought you said you were never dealing with shits from SNU.

Do you think our lives would look like this if our plans always worked out?

She was so right that I kept saying things to her boyfriend like "Damn, hyungnim," "You are so right," "You are so amazingly clever"—inane compliments like that. K3, being an engineer, had lots in common with this semiconductor specialist, and they seemed to get along, going on and on about the different cultures of their companies and technical jargon about their research. Bored with their conversation, I regaled them with tales of Jaehee's life in college, bowdlerized for this mainstream audience, of course. The dinner remains in my mind a memory of perfect propriety and respectability.

3.

Then last summer, Jaehee's boyfriend began thinking something was funny about Jieun.

—Hey Jaehee, is your roommate Jieun a cat?

—What? What are you talking about, oppa?

—She seems a little strange. Why is she always at home? Why haven't you ever introduced us? Why have I never heard her voice? And there are no photos of you together. Even a cat meows on occasion. Why haven't I ever heard her make a sound?

Thank God the relationships Jaehee had in the past were short-lived, because anyone with half a brain would've had the same suspicion. He had suggested inviting Jieun to dinner many times, but Jaehee kept saying she was shy or making up some other excuse, so of course, at some point, he would realize it was strange.

If only Jaehee could lie a bit more convincingly, then all of our lives would've been easier. Instead, the two had their first big fight ever in the year they'd been together. Bad at lying, Jaehee struggled to make up different excuses before being cornered into confessing that her "roommate Jieun" was actually a man her age. And that the roommate in question liked men.

—So, oppa, he's basically a girl. It's just like I'm living with Jieun.

—That's not the same thing! He's a man, a man is living with a woman.

Jaehee came home that evening and told me about it, her head bowed low.

—I'm really sorry. I wasn't trying to let things get this way. But they have.

—So what are you going to do about it?

I couldn't control the anger in my voice. As if she hadn't expected my reaction, Jaehee stood motionless with her head still bowed and her mouth slightly open. I wondered why my voice was shaking so much and realized: I really was angry. Even though we'd done worse things to each other. I'd dragged her drunk ass home kicking and screaming more than once, and another time she had peed on the bathroom floor by mistake, after which I had to toss her ruined stockings and scrub the floor with bleach. Then she'd wake up rubbing her eyes and say she was sorry, to which my only answer would be to give her a slap on the back and laugh out loud. But this time, I was incensed.

Betrayal.

That was something I wasn't used to feeling, given how little I expected of others.

It was funny if I thought about it. All Jaehee had done was tell the truth. Before that moment, I didn't have many hang-ups about being outed. For someone who would get drunk and immediately start kissing men in the middle of the street, it would be ridiculous to think there would be no rumors about my sexuality. But thinking of how my secret had been used as a shield in Jaehee's relationship with her boyfriend was hard to accept. I didn't care if people went around gossiping about me, but the thought of Jaehee being one of those people was intolerable. Everyone else could say whatever they wanted about me, but Jaehee should've kept her mouth shut.

Because she was Jaehee.

The things she and I shared, stories that belonged to just the two of us—I didn't want other people to know them. I believed our relationship was solely our own. Forever. So I said what I had to say.

—Don't call me.

I packed up and moved right back into my mother's apartment in the Jamsil-dong without even understanding why I'd had such an extreme reaction.

Jaehee called me a few times after, but I didn't pick up. I sent K3 a message saying I needed to think about our relationship more. He replied that he couldn't comprehend why I was always running away from him, that it was truly over between us, but every morning as the sun rose he'd drunkenly text me lines about love (plagiarized from somewhere, no doubt), misspellings and all. Jaehee on occasion sent messages saying she understood how I felt, but I had no idea what she was claiming to understand. My thoughts grew more and more poisonous in my brain, but those thoughts themselves also felt absurd to me, so I lay grinning in my childhood bed in the dark.

◊

While living in my parents' apartment, I wrote short stories. It was there that I became a writer.

Me, Jaehee, the men we met, the stories about our relationship, I mixed everything together willy-nilly, churning out my stories. I hadn't written them to show anyone. It just so happened that I was having trouble falling asleep and needed something to do, and now that I had no one to talk to all night, the thing I wanted more than anything else was to ramble on about nothing to someone. When I wrote short stories about slutty gays and lost dogs, I didn't exactly feel any satisfaction or sense of achievement. It's just that the stories I wrote and the nights I spent talking to Jaehee felt similar. I submitted a couple of the stories to a writing contest without thinking too much about what I was doing. I ended up winning.

I called Jaehee to tell her the news. Three months had passed since I'd last talked to her. Jaehee said hi as if I'd called her just three hours before, and as soon as she heard I'd won, she burst into tears. *How very you*, I thought, as I let her cry for about three minutes then read her the judges' comments. An elder novelist talked about how worried he was that my work veered into "tabloid territory." When Jaehee heard that line, she couldn't stop laughing. I used part of the prize money to buy Jaehee a Chanel lambskin bag.

I was notified of K3's death around that time. Car accident. The K3 he'd loved so much ended up becoming his coffin. Only when I heard the news did I realize I'd imagined a long stretch of time ahead where we were an *us*. This was the last line he sent me:

If obsession isn't love, I have never loved.

◊

After the funeral, I moved back into Jaehee's apartment and things seemed to return to the way they were. Jaehee stocked the freezer with blueberries just like she used to. I bought some Marlboro Reds, but she told me not to bother anymore—after cigarette prices went up, she and her boyfriend both decided to quit. Of course they did. The cigarettes I bought remained frozen and untouched.

Just like old times, we talked about our days before we went to sleep. I went on meeting the Man of the Day, and Jaehee and her boyfriend continued to avoid the Roommate/Jieun issue like it was a flagged landmine. They seemed to have decided it was like living with an embarrassing family member. But whenever he was drunk, Jaehee's boyfriend would say something along these lines:

—You do know that this situation would be unacceptable to anyone else.

Who cared? I expected them to break up one day, but the boyfriend had more stamina than I thought. Jaehee said he was more down-to-earth than anyone else she had met, and it was lovely that he always listened to what she had to say.

—He does everything I suggest, like a pet dog.

He had no weird habits, and unlike her other men, he didn't find her drinking tiresome, going so far as to joke that it was like meeting a new woman every night. (Sure it was.)

Jaehee would always fall asleep before midnight. Her work must've been draining, because she came home after ten every night and lay around the apartment like a deflated balloon, but if I messaged her saying I was close to scoring and was staying out, she'd reply like a mother waiting up for her child:

Try not to pick one who'll die before you this time.

I'll do my best.

◊

Right around then, Jaehee's boyfriend proposed to her, and she said yes. They had been going out for three years. When I heard the news, I remarked that the hyung seemed like a nice guy and all but had no eye for women. Jaehee replied, "I know, right?" And added:

—He said he loved how I would make him laugh for the rest of his life.

I hoped he didn't end up getting slapped in the back of his head for laughing so much.

But his words did make me realize that he was seeing in her the same qualities I loved. Jaehee wasn't pretty or kind, but she was definitely funny.

Still, it wasn't as if that hyung was that old—why was he in such a hurry to marry? Because he was such a congenitally down-to-earth person? From what I knew, he had an older sister who hadn't married yet . . . It did cross my mind that Jaehee's biologically male roommate may have had something to do with his decision to marry, but I decided not to think too much along those lines. Or really to think about anything that had to do with me. An excess of self-awareness being a disease in itself . . .

4.

Things moved along quickly after Jaehee announced her marriage.

For the three months before the wedding, I got to witness how shitty it was for a man and a woman in Korean society to unite as one family, which made me cease resenting the fact that I couldn't even dream of marriage. Not that I was confident it *wasn't* jealousy.

Meanwhile, Jaehee had a whole lot of things she needed from me. Her promotion came with a murderous workload, and with her future husband being largely absent from the preparations, I was her stand-in groom. I accompanied her to the bridal shop, to the hanbok shop, to interior design firms, and so on, helping her pick things out. At first, I'd only look over her shoulder as she made the decisions, but soon I was the one touching all of the fabric samples and insisting she use the colors I liked. I didn't mind it so much since it wasn't so terrible, but I drew the line when she asked me to emcee the event. No matter how much I insisted I didn't want to be involved in a straight wedding, she refused to back down.

—How could you not be a part of my wedding?

—How *could* I be a part of it? No. I refuse. I don't even own a suit.

—I'll buy you one. Armani.

—I'm an anti-marriage activist. One who's beginning to turn militant, having seen what you're going through.

—Cut the bullshit and just do it for me. You love attention!

That was a misunderstanding on her part—I was a very different man when I was drunk. But no matter how many times I declined, she kept insisting, and eventually I had to yield. Fine, I said, I'll emcee the thing, but you have to come up with the script yourself. She agreed.

Not even a week had gone by when she came home one day with two boxes of Kyochon fried chicken. Obviously, she was feeling guilty about something. Jaehee offered up the chicken and mumbled:

—So apparently, it's traditional for the groom's best friend to emcee? Oppa has a friend who's a television reporter, and he's going to do it. I'm so sorry.

Had I asked her for the role in the first place? Not that I'd ever wanted to do such a thing like emcee a wedding, but the thought of not being able to do it because of some stupid tradition disgusted me. She must've had some words with the groom. Jaehee said there was an alternate spot for me in the wedding.

—The congratulatory song.

—Are you insane?

—Think of it as paying me back for using my story to debut as a writer.

—Then give me back the Chanel bag I got you.

—If you don't do this for me, I'll sue your publisher for defamation.

Public embarrassment seemed a better choice than a lawsuit, and with the successful negotiation of adding an Armani suit and shirt and a Gucci necktie to the bargain, I was all set to sing for her wedding.

The newlyweds were to live in an apartment in the Bangeui-dong neighborhood. Jaehee's parents had apparently bought it years ago as an investment.

◊

On our last day of living together, we bought ten of the largest-size boxes at the post office. We neatly packed them with Jaehee's stuff, like her shift dresses and leather jacket. Jaehee said to me:

—Young-ah, do you think I'll be able to keep myself from cheating on him?

—Well.

—I don't really worry about oppa, but I worry about myself. That I might ruin a perfectly fine man.

—You know, Jaehee . . . I worry about that, too.

We laughed and finished packing up. There was less stuff than we expected, and we ended up using only five boxes. She told me she had already sent on her winter clothes and furniture to the apartment. There were five months left on the lease for our studio apartment, and Jaehee was letting me live out the rest of it alone. The jeonse deposit was a big chunk of money, but seeing as how she wasn't in a rush to claim it, Jaehee's family must've been well-off, perhaps even more so than her fiancé's. I began to wonder if Jaehee really was the ordinary middle-class girl I had thought she was, someone just like everyone else. Maybe that's why she could toss societal norms like used Kleenex . . .

After we were done, we spread out the bedding and lay down with facial masks on our faces, feeling like we were nineteen again. It was still surreal to me to think that the vagabond that Jaehee used to be was now all grown up and getting married.

—So do you think you can really take care of your in-laws and have babies and change their diapers and everything?

—I wrote up a whole contract with oppa. That we're never going to have babies. As for the in-laws, well, I'm going to think of it as having two more birthdays to take care of. We're going to keep on living like we're dating.

—Then why not just keep on dating? Why get married?

—He suggested it, so I thought I might as well try it. And if it doesn't work out, I can always leave.

—Yeah. If it gets to be too much, ditch him and come back here.

—Do you think I wouldn't?

—You've come all this way because you know you wouldn't.

That's what I said, but there was no reply. Instead, a boisterous snoring. Jaehee's careless catchphrase, "Or not," was reverberating in my head; it used to drive me up the wall, but now it felt reassuring.

Jaehee was the one getting married, but I was the one who couldn't fall asleep. And so, our last night together wore on.

5.

The emcee called my name, announcing me as the singer for the congratulatory song.

My whole university cohort turned their heads toward me. Some burst out in incredulous laughter. I got up from the immaculately set table and slowly moved toward the stage. My shoulders were stiff from nerves. Jaehee and her groom were smiling widely at me. Hundreds of wedding guests were staring. Intimidated by their glares, I gripped the microphone tight. The lyrics on the music stand in front of me were swimming before my eyes. Why did grabbing a microphone always have this effect on me? As a writer I had had to do some events speaking into a microphone, and I always ended up saying too much or suddenly bursting into tears at a random moment, startling the audience. My inner drama queen had surprised me on more than a few occasions.

I heard the intro. Melon Music had been offering the instrumental track for 1,000 won, which for some reason annoyed me so much that I purchased a different, 700-won version, but it sounded tinnier than a karaoke track. Tears threatened any moment—I concentrated all my power on my nose. *Don't do this. You've got to endure it. Press it down.* I bit my trembling lower lip. At least three of the guests were men Jaehee had slept with, and there were even two in the audience who I'd slept with. (Putting an ironic spin on the "minority" in "sexual minorities.") Jaehee and her groom, in their caked-on wedding makeup, gazed at me as they smiled their fake smiles.

In the end, I failed to sing the song properly. I managed to muddle through the first verse and chorus in my shaky voice, but in the second verse, everything fell apart.

Stay with me always, I want you to be the keeper of my dreams—I tried to get myself to that point at least. *Jaehee, you're really leaving me behind*. The people who had stifled their laughter at the intro were letting it loose for real when I turned my head away in the middle of the song, thinking that I was acting a part and hamming it up. Then Jaehee came over to me, dragging the train of her dress, and took the microphone. She began singing the rest of the song.

—The only one in my heart, that one precious love . . .

Jaehee could do anything, but she was a terrible singer, and the backing track was for male voices, making her sound even worse. The elegance of the hotel wedding took a nosedive into the black carpeting and my tears went right back inside their ducts, making me marvel at how Jaehee would always be on brand. I sucked in my snot and finished the rest of the song with her, thinking that I was all right with losing to anyone in the world but her, that the Ock Joo-hyun of the day was going to be *me*. I sang with all my heart.

When I got back to my seat, my cohort was laughing it up and saying, "Who listens to Fin.K.L in this day and age?" "You weren't really crying just now, were you?" *I'm a faggot so I'm going to sing Fin.K.L*, I almost said but didn't. Instead, I chewed my way through the steak that had gone cold. Everyone else at my table had so much stuff to talk about. Who was next to get married, who had just had a baby, who had gotten a promotion, who had switched companies, who had failed to get a job, who had inherited a holiday home from their parents . . . Noisy, boring chatter, so effortlessly generated. That Jaehee's new apartment was in Songpa, that it had appreciated in value by 300 million won, that Jaehee had met a rich guy and had basically won the lottery . . . I wanted to say it was *her* parents who bought the apartment, you morons . . . but I didn't. Why bother? I got up from my seat with the steak half eaten. Saying I was going to the bathroom, I walked out of the hotel.

As soon as I got home, I threw off my suit jacket. I stripped completely naked and lay down on the bed. That was something I could never do when Jaehee and I lived together. How nice and cool it was to live alone. The sun hadn't even set, but lying there like that made me feel like I'd drunk a lot and was greeting the dawn naked. Since I had the place to myself, I thought of inviting a guy over, but I couldn't be bothered in the end. With the sunlight shimmering outside the window, out of habit I flicked through my text messages. Tedious notifications of credit card transactions, spam texts, Jaehee begging me to forgive her. Then, the last text that K3 had sent me.

If obsession isn't love, I have never loved.

I dropped my phone. For a moment I thought I might shower, but then I craved something cold. Inside the freezer was an almost empty bag of blueberries and a pack of Marlboro Reds with the cellophane still intact. I stared for a long time at the photo of a man's rotten lung on the packet. This man . . . was he dead now? I took out a bowl from the cabinet and flipped the blueberry bag over it. All that came out of it were tiny shards of purple ice.

That's when I realized that my time with Jaehee, which I thought would last forever, was over.

She had always stocked the fridge with blueberries. Remembered the names and faces of every man I'd slept with, been the external backup drive of my love life. Smoking everywhere, meeting the most unsuitable men.

Jaehee, who had taught me that every season is its own beautiful moment—that Jaehee didn't live here anymore.

PART TWO

A Bite of Rockfish, Taste the Universe

1.

I spent all night writing and overslept the next morning, so I only had time to splash my face with water and grab my work bag before heading out of the door. Umma would probably be reading her Bible, trying to suppress her irritation at having woken up in a hospital room yet again. I would see her in a few hours. We'd settled into a routine in which she and I had lunch together before taking a walk in Olympic Park.

On my way down the steps I glanced at my letterbox out of habit and saw a manila folder stuffed into the opening. I took it out, feeling the thickness between my fingers. There was no return address. *What the hell?* I ripped it open. A ream of yellowed paper was inside.

The writing I had more or less thrown in his face five years before: my diary.

Feeling like I was standing naked in front of a mirror, I started to read the first page. There were red editorial marks over the black letters of my whip-like writing, and underlining that marked awkward expressions. In other words, the bastard had sent me an edit of my diary. Not five days after receiving it, but five years. My fingers gripped the paper as memories of him poured into me like a violent flood. He still remembered my address? The writing on the last page was not my rapid scrawl but a note in his handwriting. It looked as though it were written in blood.

Hello. It's hyung. I heard you've become a writer. Congratulations. I thought your real name had a "je" in it, am I right? You must be using a pseudonym.

This idiot. He couldn't even remember the name of someone he'd gone out with for over a year.

You've gained so much weight that I didn't recognize you at first.

Fuck it. I've read enough. Tear this shit up. But then, the next sentence:

I wonder if your mother's doing better now. I'm sorry about before. About a lot of things. All of it.

Why do men always apologize to me? Just don't do the thing that will make you apologize in the first place. Then, just as he always did, he went on talking about himself.

I thought of contacting you many times in the past, but I had my own reasons not to. Then too much time passed, and you changed your phone number, as one does. I apologize for contacting you all of a sudden. I was just so busy. I'm leaving the country on Monday. For a long time. I may not come back. If it is all right, I would like to see you this Sunday. The same place and time we promised before. There's something I would very much like to give to you.

He included his phone number at the end. Sunday. That was in two days. A little presumptuous of him to ask for a meeting at all, much less with such short notice. And forget this "giving me something" crap. All we had left to exchange were insults. I was torn between shoving the envelope and its contents into the trash and putting it carefully away somewhere no one would ever find it. In the end, I stuffed it into my bag.

My heart was racing as I walked down the street. I was shocked and humiliated that he could still provoke such a visceral response from me. I took out my phone, opened the notepad app where I started story drafts, and typed a single sentence.

Five years ago, I tried to introduce him to my mother.

◊

Thankfully, my mother was still asleep, snoring. She must've dozed off right after lunch. I quietly stepped inside, slid the caregiver bed out from underneath hers, and sat down.

Umma's things began to multiply in the hospital room as she kept extending her stay. Side dishes and fruit in the fridge, a fruit knife in a drawer, a bag of peppermint candies, a little framed picture on the nightstand. The picture was of me at ten and her at thirty-eight. Umma wore the cap from a graduation gown and stood next to some statue, and I stood next to her wearing denim overalls and a sour expression. Every photo of me from around that time has me frowning. Maybe I was born with a shitty attitude. Next to the photo were copies of the two books I had published this year. They were for visitors; Umma never read my books. In fact, she'd never read a single word I'd published—a denial that bordered on the obsessive. She claimed it was because her aging eyes made every letter look like a tiger about to pounce, but I knew there was a different reason.

When I was nineteen, I won a literary prize given out by a college newspaper. The winner would get a million won in scholarship money, and a friend who was on staff happened to pass onto me that there were very few applicants that year. I was always short on money for drinks, so I wrote about a woman in her fifties who'd always had an inferiority complex about her education, who went on to get two bachelor's degrees at an online university and threw everything she had into her son's education; it was the only story I could write at that time, and the judges declared it the winner on the strength of its "dynamic rendering of its main character." Umma heard the news (from her church, no doubt, the source of all evil rumor in this world), got a copy of the paper, and read the story. Then she cried for four days straight. I could hear her sobs and lamentations through her bedroom door. "I can't believe I hurt you so much, I can't believe I exploited you like that!" "Umma, for God's sake, fiction is just fiction! It's all made up!" She refused to listen to me and from then on avoided anything I wrote, even notes or school reports I dropped on the living room floor.

—Myoung-hee loved your book. She said she's read everything you've published so far. You know she's the smartest of all my friends. A Sookdae grad, no less. She said your writing made her think you'd grown up into a very fine young man.

The fiction I'd put out over the past three years was all about getting drunk, stealing things, illegally committing homosexual acts in the military, prostitution, cheating on boyfriends—what on earth was in there to cast the author as "a fine young man"?! If he was any finer, he'd murder someone. In any case, you had to hand it to the church ladies—they really were consummate spin doctors.

Umma paused her patented soft snoring and sat up, complaining about how she hadn't slept well the previous night. Yawning, she mentioned that the pain from chemotherapy made it hard for her to sleep. Her snoring had already scared off two previous roommates, so for better or worse she'd had the two-person room all to herself for the past three months. Before, she'd complained about having to share a room, but now she ranted in a most un-Christian, shamanistic way, for someone who had devoted the past forty years of her life to her church, about Death coming to visit her in the night.

—Umma, do you want me to peel an apple for you?

—There's a bitterness in my mouth. Unwrap a candy for me instead.

She had never eaten sweet things in her life, but ever since her tumor removal surgery, all she craved was peppermint drops. I once made her spit out her candy when I found her picking at her lunch. They said her digestive system was unable to work properly. I sprayed Febreze on the sheets to cover up that sickly hospital-ward smell.

Five months ago, I'd been dismayed but not surprised to learn that Umma's cancer had returned. She'd been in remission for years, but I had been worried it might come back. And I was sick of this repetition of joy and pain, comedy and tragedy—nothing good ever came of it. I'd already been through everything the relative of a cancer patient could possibly experience, except the funeral. And perhaps now it was time to prepare for this final step as well.

◊

It had been six years since the cancer was first discovered in my mother's body.

I was an intern in my mid-twenties. The ten interns who had started out had been whittled down to three. Rumor had it that only one would score a permanent contract, and as the only male remaining, it was likely to be me. The research team I assisted investigated the correlation between political leanings and the health of people in their fifties, calling over a hundred people a day. But it was truly a first when a certain center-right woman in her fifties called *me* out of the blue. I hung up on her twice, but she refused to stop calling. I ended up sneaking in a call though the company phone.

—Hello, I'm calling from Korea Research—

Umma interrupted me, her voice filled with joy.

—Your mother has cancer! In the uterus! Hallelujah.

She was so excited about it, you'd have thought she'd won the lottery instead of being diagnosed with cancer. Two weeks ago, she'd had a dream about azaleas blooming in her stomach and had had "a bad feeling," leading her to get a check-up, where she learned she had uterine cancer. Several of the church ladies sold insurance, and the various cancer policies she'd taken out so as to stay on their good side were due to pay out over 200 million won—enough money to pay off the mortgage on our Jamsil-dong apartment. Umma seemed genuinely happy as she went on about how the surgery costs were being reimbursed through the cancer insurance, explaining that we would come out in the black thanks to the rent we collected from the retail units in Suwon and Anyang. She added that because she, my grandmother, and my aunt all had cancer, I was sure to get it myself, and happily proposed that I take out two cancer policies in my name.

My boss was curious as to why I was quitting.

—Did you get a job at a better company?

No, my mother is a widow with cancer, she needs someone to take care of her, was what I wanted to say, but I didn't. Umma liked to keep things to herself, even things there was no real need to hide, because it was "common" to let others know your business. Her extroverted personality concealed how uncomfortable she was with shame, and she seemed to be very ashamed of her sickness. She fobbed off the clients she'd been managing for twenty years with a story about taking a sabbatical to tour the Holy Land; not even her friends or my aunts were let in on the secret. I had no idea what was so shameful about cancer, but I went along with her wishes all the same. And that's why, to my boss's question, I smiled and said I was planning on becoming a writer after I quit. I even added that it had been my lifelong dream.

—Dreams are all well and good. But remember this: opportunities are like trains. Once you miss one, it will never come again.

Is this guy a fucking idiot, doesn't he know trains come again and again like clockwork? In any case, I quit my job, and two weeks later my mother lay down on the operating table of a Gangnam hospital said to specialize in uterine cancer, where she asked the doctors not to anesthetize her because she wanted to participate in the pain of Jesus Christ, a declaration that (finally!) prompted her doctors to add some psychiatric treatment to her prescription.

Umma's cancer, which the X-rays had shown as minor, turned out to be serious once they opened her up. The surgeon suspected that it had metastasized to the lymph nodes, and the liver function also seemed impaired. He recommended a multistep treatment implemented over a longer period of time. Despite multiple bouts of radiation after her hysterectomy, the cancer cells were slow to disappear. The road to remission turned out to be long and difficult.

It was around then when I first met him, in a humanities class at a private institute. The reason I picked the class on "The Philosophy of Emotions" was because I was having a hard time keeping a lid on my feelings. Not only was I cramming for English aptitude tests and entrance exams for companies, I was also taking care of Umma at the hospital and going with her for a daily walk after she had first begged for and then demanded it. Taking care of someone who was thoroughly sick in both body and mind made me feel like I was coming down with something myself. Hoping to avoid the well of unhappiness that was my mother, and to understand the feelings that kept threatening to boil over, I went to the class once a week. The course used Spinoza's *Ethics* as a textbook and Roland Barthes's *Camera Lucida* and *A Lover's Discourse* as supplementary texts, dividing up classes by different emotions. The instructor, who introduced himself as a "freelance philosopher," did what most inexperienced teachers do, which was to force everyone to go around introducing themselves to the class. The school being run by a human rights organization, half of the students were activists. They went on about their affiliations, political beliefs, and sexual orientations (not that anyone had asked them), and I felt the pressure to confess to being a "center-left male homosexual" when my turn came, but I just stated my real name and that I was a college student. Jo Wind, James, Mapsosa, Legend of the Fall . . . The others had activist nicknames of bizarre national origins and esoteric references.

Someone came in the door just as the last person had finished introducing themselves. He was so tall that his head almost touched the ceiling, which explained why he had a slight stoop. He put his bag down on the seat next to me and shrugged off his hoodie. Both the black hoodie and the Eastpak backpack, which had a South Korean flag sewn into it, looked a few decades old. He must've been running, because the heat from his body slammed into my face. I saw hints of what seemed like a long tattoo on his neck, wrists, and even fingers. Something like a lizard's tail. I wondered what shape would emerge if I followed it, or where that journey would end. I found myself gulping down saliva as my eyes took in every inch of him. Before I knew what was happening, he was right by my side. I felt the little hairs on my body stand up, all the way from my ears to my toes. He put his mouth next to my ear and whispered:

—Uh, excuse me, but could I have a sip of your coffee?

Before I could even reply, he popped the plastic lid off the disposable cup in front of me and started chugging down the iced Americano. I perceived his movements in slow motion. He clearly didn't give a damn about my (no doubt steaming) gaze as he drank the whole thing down to the ice, which he then crunched between his teeth. For his introduction, he said he was "a creative" and left it at that. In that teeth-chillingly cool, simple declaration, in which he neglected to mention the field of this "creativity," I had an inauspicious foreboding that this man was seriously full of himself (a feeling that soon proved to be accurate).

After the class was over, the man came up to me and offered to buy me a coffee, to pay me back for the one he'd drunk earlier. The fact he had taken my coffee without permission gave me a bad feeling, not to mention his way of talking and the look in his eye—so I waved away his offer. He then said, very formally, that he wanted to repay me for the moral good I'd done. That we then proceeded to walk to a nearby Starbucks wasn't because I couldn't again refuse such a moral offer but because in fact he was actually totally my type. He had a low, clear voice, a prominent brow, unreadably thin lips, and freckled skin that had never known the touch of sunscreen. His personality seemed a little weird, but the anticipation of spending a few minutes gazing at the good-looking guy overwhelmed all foreboding (again, in hindsight, a mistake).

Standing there at the counter, I noticed that he was a head taller than I was. It was unusual for me to have to look up at someone, my own height being slightly above average. We took up our iced Americanos and found a seat. He'd been the one to suggest coffee, but now he was just sitting there silently and staring into space.

What is up with this guy? Why did he ask me out if he was going to just say nothing?

In the end, I was the one who had to grope for an opener.

—You must've been very thirsty.

—You saved my life.

And . . . silence. Back then, as a temp who dreamed of a permanent contract, I was all about "putting myself out there," which meant babbling on (entirely unprompted) about how I was a college student, majoring in French, how my favorite hobby was reading, how I had joined this class because . . . I kept on talking about whatever pointless crap came into my head. Meanwhile, the man stared at me almost rudely, as if sizing me up, and finally opened his mouth just when I was starting to run out of steam.

—You have a pretty way of talking.

What the hell is he saying, this guy, that I'm faggy? That I sound gay? Or is he just saying stuff for the hell of it? Am I being paranoid? Too many thoughts, which made me shut up. More silence. After an awkward pause had built up long enough for me to see the bottom of my mug, he suddenly piped up again.

—My umma is an alcoholic.

—Uh . . . OK?

—So I put her into rehab, but she escaped so many times that we've had to try a psychiatric facility.

—Uh . . . OK.

—We keep changing treatments but there's no progress. She always finds a way to hide the alcohol. There are bottles under her bed, in her bag. It drives me crazy.

Who talks about their mother's alcoholism to someone they've just met? How was I supposed to react?

—She's even showing signs of early Alzheimer's brought on by alcohol poisoning. It's getting harder and harder to deal with her. Every four days or so she escapes from the ward, and I have to chase her around the hospital trying to catch her.

Jesus, what is wrong with this guy? Just how weird is he?

I felt a sudden pressure to lay out my own family saga. *Our family is extremely ordinary, and like any ordinary patriarch, my father had so many affairs that my mother eventually divorced him, my mother is now suffering from the number one killer of middle-aged Koreans, aka cancer*—was that what I ought to say at this point? Or should I come up with something even more elaborate? In the end, I stuck to the basics.

—My umma is sick, too. Uterine cancer. She's been hospitalized, and I'm taking care of her.

—Ah, I see. We have a lot in common.

It hit me that this was the first time I'd mentioned my mother's sickness to someone else. The man spoke again.

—This is your first time taking a class at the institute, right?

—Yes. How did you know?

—I've taken almost every humanities and philosophy class there. I'd never seen your face before. I'd remember such a cute face.

I still remember his expression when he said this. He acted all cool and nonchalant, but his trembling eyes and the hesitation in his lips showed how nervous he was. I was taken aback. No one had ever called me cute, not even as a joke, at least not since I was a baby. My complete and utter un-cuteness was the key to my cuteness, at best. Was he flirting with me? Was this some kind of (very unsmooth) courtship situation? That couldn't be right. I had a mirror at home, I knew all too well that I wasn't worth a whole cup of coffee. I was so stumped, I couldn't think of anything to say. I was trembling and was so nervous I couldn't look him in the eye, and I was trying my best to hide it. Then, in a tone so light as to mock me, he added:

—If you don't have anything to do after class, let's have dinner together each week.

And so we ended up wandering around the area after each class, picking a place to have dinner. He was the one who knew the shops and restaurants well, introducing me to all the hot spots (which mostly served rice and side dishes, the kind of homestyle places frequented by middle-aged men), while I luxuriated in the false sense of being invited into his intimate spaces (I later learned that he liked pretending to be knowledgeable to any random person).

When I was with him, I became someone who spoke and ate little. I was completely intent on observing him, squirreling away within myself the sight of his short, unkempt hair, the warm air that flowed between his front teeth when he laughed, the way he raised an eyebrow when he felt shy, and the slight whistle whenever he pronounced an *s*. After dinner, I had to scramble to keep up with him on my at-least-four-inches-shorter legs as he strode along with his gaze straight ahead. I was often thrown into despair over the fact that he never once looked back at me on that long walk to the subway station.

Whenever I sat staring at him, all kinds of thoughts ran through my head. I wanted to know him as a person, and more than that to know what he thought of me, and even more than that, I longed to understand how he managed to keep jerking my emotions around. My thoughts, my feelings kept racing ahead at hundreds of miles per second, and I hadn't a clue as to what to do with this kind of energy. So, I turned the spiralbound notebook I had bought for the class into a diary and wrote about him and the changes in my emotions that he brought on, recording and examining my feelings.

The more I wrote, the less I understood.

He shared very little about his life, but I knew he did not have a job that demanded regular hours, and he seemed to meet up with almost no one apart from me. From time to time he sent me meaningless text messages (*Today is a good day for a walk*) and articles about foods that were good for your immune system and battling cancer, much like an old uncle. These would spark a conversation that covered his very boring day (*Today I read Kant and fed some stray cats*), the situation with his alcoholic mother (*She escaped from the hospital, got a hold of some alcohol, and fought with a taxi driver*), and photos of his one-person dinners (*I cooked some spicy mackerel*). To these I barely managed to reply meaningless answers like *Ah, yes; How bad for you; Have a nice meal.* If the conversation threatened to break off because of my lackluster replies, he sent smiley-face emojis or fat-cat stickers to prolong our awkward exchange. A few more meaningless messages and my mood would end up like a deflated balloon, with me believing that he wasn't talking to me because he was interested in me (for whatever reason), but that he was simply so lonely it was either talk to me or talk to the walls. I knew the temperature and the smell of such loneliness all too well.

Because back then I was exactly the same kind of person.

2.

One Saturday afternoon, when my mother had just finished her Healing Yoga session, she goaded me into taking another walk together. It was the same route we always took, but my mood was a different shade than usual. That ream of paper he had sent me had completely upended my life. My emotions were swinging up one second and down the next, just like they had five years ago. I couldn't concentrate or do any work. I sent an email to my publisher asking for a week's extension on my next manuscript.

Umma and I headed for Olympic Park. It was just across the street from the hospital. She leaned on me, and we crossed the street slowly, arm in arm. From afar, we probably looked like a mother-son pair on very good terms. As on any other day, we talked for about ten minutes before sitting down on a bench near the reservoir.

I'd been told that survival rates were lower for cancers that returned. The second time around, it was easier to let go. Neither mother nor son was alarmed when we were told that they were taking out part of her liver and biliary tract where the cancer had metastasized, or when Umma had to go through her fifth round of treatment, or when we heard she had less than a 20 percent chance of living for another year. I had to again quit the company I was working for. My boss told me to come back if things ever got better, but I was thirty years old now, no longer naive enough to believe such promises.

The long-term care hospital where Umma was now staying was about fifteen minutes from home. She had been in a different hospital, on the outskirts of Gyeonggi Province, for half a year, but we had moved her when a lung cancer patient around her age whom she had been close to had suddenly passed away. I guess the new hospital was more of a hospice. The wards, the facilities, everything was as immaculate as a hotel. Professional caretakers and healers provided round-the-clock care that included mainstream and alternative medicines, and I had much less to do once Umma moved there. The fees were much more than my monthly salary, but I thought that we should spend our last days together in a place where she was most comfortable. Umma gave up fighting against her cancer and instead received alternative treatments for her pain while diligently taking up yoga and mindful meditation. Her cancer, being equally diligent, spread all over her body. The areas and forms of her pain kept changing by the day.

Umma told me she needed to go to the bathroom. I took her to the disabled booth in the public bathroom, sat her down on the toilet, and turned away. Ever since the cancer had spread to her bladder, she'd been complaining of increased pain when she urinated. Getting up from bed or coughing, any action that put pressure on her stomach, gave her so much pain that she had to call for my assistance. I stared at the bathroom door as I listened to the weak trickle of her going to the bathroom. I'd been in this situation several times before, but I still couldn't get used to it. Umma seemed unperturbed despite death's being so close and all. She simply grabbed the toilet paper from my hand, wiped herself, and pulled up her underwear and trousers. While I closed my eyes and took care of the rest of it, she remarked, "I should've had a daughter," a sentiment thirty years too late. She left me standing there bemused while striding off on her own, confident as anything. You wouldn't believe she'd had trouble using the toilet on her own just a moment ago. Outside, all the while exclaiming how refreshing the air was, she clapped her hands hard to aid her circulation, a sound so loud I thought the dirt path would lift itself off the ground.

—What are you talking about? The air quality report says fine-dust levels are well over a hundred today, that's "Very Bad" according to the app.

The cancer hadn't seemed to have affected her lungs or breathing, thank God. Umma saw my annoyed expression and launched into one of her rants.

—I washed all of your shitty diapers while I raised you, I don't know why you're making such a fuss about a little pee now. Well, what else would I expect from you? You were just like this when your grandmother had cancer. When you could barely walk, you crawled to where she was lying down and slapped her in the face! I would put you down somewhere and you would still go and slap her. If I closed the door on you, you'd push it open to go and slap her. That was the kind of kid you were. A mean little bastard.

—Jesus, when are you going to stop talking about that?

—When I die, why?

She'd played the death card so many times that I was pretty sure I'd predecease her from the sheer repetition. In a voice too loud for anyone who'd been informed of how many days they had left in this world, she shouted that I should "do better by your mother while she's still alive, this is all for your own good!" This rant, once begun, segued into how I was never getting married. She pretended to ask after my friend Jaehee, who had recently found a husband, about some acquaintance's son who already had two sons of his own, and about some former bachelor who'd been a complete idiot before getting married and was now buying an apartment in Pangyo—her same old repertoire from beginning to end. I was sick of this lament for marriage, but I could understand where she was coming from. This particular drive was how she had kept me fed and sheltered throughout my whole childhood.

When I was eleven, Umma bravely divorced my father, who had not only stepped out of their marriage numerous times but also bankrupted his business. Suddenly the new head of the household, Umma got a job as a couples manager at a Scandinavian matchmaking company that had just opened a Korean branch and was struggling with personnel issues. The matchmaking industry in the late nineties (consisting mostly of "Madame Du" freelance matchmakers) was hit hard when the sophisticated Scandinavian system arrived on the market. Umma carried a bag full of charts on members' schooling, professions, fortunes, height, weight, and ranking of looks (how would you even . . . ?), everything quantified and stratified by percentile. On the back of the charts were results of personality tests, like the Enneagram or the MBTI. Through this system, the most appropriate match according to social conditions and personalities would be found. The market really took off when men and women from the affluent Gangnam and Songpa districts, who had almost ended up forever single after the upheavals of the Asian financial crisis of the late nineties, began turning their attention to the idea of marriage. Umma used her disarming personality, her wide-ranging connections, and her societal sensibilities to quickly rise in the ranks as a popular "couples manager" and was able to strike out on her own in less than three years. Later, she entered an online degree program in psychology, determined to become the absolute best in her field. She plagiarized the psychology charts used by her previous employer, adding a few categories and moving around a couple more to conceal the theft, set up an unregistered company she called "Hatfield Korea" (a pseudo Western name that sounded like it could belong to a famous psychiatrist), and created business cards for herself that fraudulently proclaimed her to be a "psychological counselor." I remember how, when I was little, she would slap me on my back for scribbling on the backs of her charts with crayons. As long as the unmarried men and women of Gangnam ate steak and pasta and drank coffee and tea on their arranged dates, my flesh and bones grew too, just as they should. Umma was absolutely convinced in those days that if our family put its best foot forward, we could end up in society's top percentile and live the dream of a beautiful Scandinavian lifestyle.

I was the first to give this dream the boot. Once I reached puberty, I realized that I was not the kind of person who was tolerated within a Christian family system. There was also a certain incident: when I was in high school, Umma caught me kissing a science-track student two years older than me.

It happened in that most clichéd of places, the apartment complex's playground at night. Two high school boys with shorn heads were kissing beneath the spotlight of the streetlamps, watched by a middle-aged woman. Namely: my mother, who had become an evangelical Christian twenty-five years earlier. I'd been caught so red-handed there was no room for excuses. Unlike someone in a television drama, Umma did not drop her bag in surprise or scream or cry. She simply turned away as if nothing had happened and went into the apartment.

The next day, instead of criticizing or punishing me, she put me in her tiny red car. Then, she drove me to a psychiatric center in Yangju, Gyeonggi Province, where she had me forcefully hospitalized. When I protested and tried to turn back, she grabbed my wrist, her eyes filled with sincere warmth.

—As your mother, all I can see is the rage flooding your heart. Don't worry. Umma won't let you suffer like this.

That's how I was put under lock and key. Every morning I was administered a blood test, among other exams, and I had to take more than eight pills with each meal. Afternoons were mostly spent in therapy. The hospital building was old and its air-conditioning bad, my crotch and armpits were frequently drenched from sweat, but without any deodorant or shower gel, there were many days when I just sat in my own smell. I shared my room with a forty-eight-year-old man named Kim Hyeondong, who had trouble controlling his anger and minor schizophrenia. He talked to himself a lot when awake and snored loudly when asleep. He also farted a lot, maybe as a side effect of his medication, and that pushed me over the edge—thanks to my sensitive hearing. Plus, the old screen over the window was riddled with holes, so the mosquitoes made a proper night's sleep impossible. If I did manage to fall asleep, my vivid dreams meant I never really rested.

In my dreams, there was always a woman. A woman with her hair tied up in a bun, who drove a small red car. She was driving with her eyes closed. The car went faster and faster. *You seem to have a long way to go. How busy you must be.*

When I woke, I was as tired as if I'd been driving all night. The fifteen days of examinations and consultations brought the psychiatrist in charge to one conclusion: that I exhibited trauma symptoms similar to those of someone who had gone to war. The cognitive therapist came to a similar conclusion. For sixteen years (my whole life), I had been subjugated to the force of my mother's will, so I had repressed my psychological needs for all that time. The psychiatrist, after hearing everything that had gone on between me and my mother, concluded that it was my mother who needed urgent psychiatric attention, not me. I was allowed to leave the facility, so long as I was under supervision of a guardian.

On the day she drove me back to Seoul in her red car, Umma handed me a note.

Leviticus 20:13. If a man has sexual relations with a man as one does with a woman, both of them have done what is detestable. They are to be put to death; their blood will be on their own heads.

—I hope you're feeling much better.

—Apparently you're the one who's sick, not me. The doctor said so.

Things with the science-track student had cooled off by the time I got back. My old cell phone had been thrown away and the new cell had only my mother's number stored. "It's been handled," was all she said to me, her office-speak matched by her businesslike manner.

After two sessions, Umma refused to undergo further consultations or to take any medication. She turned down the hospital's offer to change her therapist. She said there was no need. She had already been redeemed by Jesus, and therefore the situation had been handled. When I heard this from the doctor, I had to ask Umma a question.

—Are you sure you won't regret it later on?

She gave me a blank, nonjudgmental look, like she would give to a bit of empty air in front of her. But then:

—Don't tell anyone. It's a shameful thing.

Kissing a boy two years older than me? Spending my summer vacation imprisoned in a psychiatric hospital because of it? Surviving sixteen years with a mother like her? I didn't know which was supposed to be so shameful, and so I ended up keeping all these secrets to myself.

Having learned to give up and accept things in silence, I went back to my routine college-prep life after the end of summer vacation. I'm sure I looked ordinary and unremarkable to others, but I was keeping to myself a dark, toxic promise I'd made to the sixteen-year-old boy I was in that psychiatric hospital: when that woman I lived with under the same roof was old and weak, I would leave her out in some neglected forest of Gyeonggi Province so she'd be eaten by starving wild animals. And the only reason I survived those years was because I had repeated that same promise to myself, over and over.

I never should have abandoned that promise.

I guess she hadn't had a good night's sleep or something. Her marriage lament this time around was especially long and tedious. Umma was an expert at latching onto the tiniest thing and spinning it into an endless, irritating rant.

—How can you be in your thirties already and never have brought home a girl?

—I'm not seeing anyone.

—You said you were, before.

—That was five years ago, Umma. There's no one now.

The "before" Umma referred to was him. The man who had been by my side but was now completely gone from my life. Except for this sudden reappearance in my letterbox, as if Umma had something to do with bringing him back from oblivion.

Oh Umma, you should've been a shaman, not a Madame Du. Then you'd own a whole building, not just a tiny bit of retail space.

◊

The fourth class in the Philosophy of Emotions was about "the feeling of completely immersing oneself in something."

Afterwards, he took me out for hwe. He said he'd pay for the fish if I got the alcohol. This was the perfect proposal, as I'd never refused alcohol or raw fish in my life. I sat across from him, determined as ever not to show my feelings for him until I understood how he felt about me. He must've been a regular, because a "medium set," including flounder, rockfish, and spicy fish soup, appeared before us without anyone having to take our order. I added two bottles of soju. Behind him were several fish tanks. They must've sold out that evening, because the tanks were empty except for little bubbles from the circulation system. The aquarium tanks were backlighting him, and the effect was somewhat creepy. He wiped his hands with the wet wipes provided and stared off into space. His thick fingers with their snake-like tattoo, his almost hairless wrists, biceps, and triceps, his small earlobes, the curve of his ear, and his firm jawline—my eyes roamed all over his body, until they met his own. I quickly looked away and asked a question I wasn't even that curious about.

—Why did you take so many philosophy classes?

—I'm very interested in how the world works.

—A laudably broad interest for a "creative."

Silence. Anxiety had caused me to blurt out whatever came to mind, and I was regretting having come across as rude. But he didn't seem to care—he looked as though he was considering his next words carefully, poised to reveal some great secret.

—Actually, I'm working on a philosophy book.

—What?

—I'm an editor at a publisher that puts out books on theory. Or I used to be. Now I'm a subcontractor at the same company.

—Uh . . . OK.

He had such an unexpectedly normal job that I was surprised to the point of rudeness. I should've known. All the paper inside his backpack, the sewn-on Korean flag, the fine felt-tip pens in red and black, plus the pre-sharpened pencils in the pencil case—these were all items that screamed "editor at a book publisher." Like most revelations, this one came way too late.

—But really, I've always been interested in the universe. It's curious. Why the world looks the way it does, why there are so many stars in the wide, vast sky, and how pitifully absurd I am, that kind of thing.

—Yes. Human beings are absurd. Pitifully so.

Although not as absurd as his philosophy, apparently. He sighed deeply and added one more thing in a somewhat overly serious tone.

—Thinking about it makes me very lonely.

His eyes did look very lonely, it was true. I didn't know what to say. All of the social skills I'd mastered during my twenty-five years on Earth seemed useless, so the only thing to do was apply myself to the raw flounder hwe in front of me, my chopsticks conveying the morsels of fish to my mouth at an almost competitive speed. He had his chopsticks up against his lips as he looked at me, smiling. *Is there something in my teeth, why are you looking at me when I'm eating?*

—What do you think you're eating now?

—Flounder. Wait, is this rockfish? I can't really tell fish apart. I just like whatever's expensive.

—You're right and wrong. You're eating rockfish right now, but what you're tasting isn't rockfish. The taste on the tip of your tongue is the taste of the universe.

—What? What (*bullshit*) are you talking about?

—The rockfish that we eat, and our own bodies, these are all part of the universe. Therefore, we're universes tasting the universe.

—Uh . . .

—Each of us is a universe and, as part of the larger universe, we live and move and have relations with each other—isn't that fascinating?

Now that I thought about it, his gaze did look a little unfocused. Was he part of some cult? I suddenly remembered hearing about all the weirdos who drifted into extension courses like ours. I had one hand gripping my bag in case I needed to make a run for it, but he didn't seem about to drag me off by the scruff of my neck to a meeting. And now that the topic of conversation had reached the existential matters of the universe, there was nowhere else for it to go. My gaze drifted back to the tattoo on his fingers, and when he noticed me looking, he quickly tried to draw his sleeve down to hide it.

—I like your tattoo. I've been wondering about it since the first time I saw it. About what it might be.

—Actually, I was in a motorcycle accident in high school. I got the tattoo done to cover the scars.

—Oh, I see.

—It's not like I was wild or anything back then.

—I can see that.

Unable to bear the silence that felt heavier than the universe, I ended up downing all the soju we'd ordered. He must've thought I needed more to drink because he kept refilling my glass as he sipped his own, and with all the fish and the pouring of each other's shots, our faces soon became red.

—The more transparent one is the flounder.

—Excuse me?

—The more transparent one of the two is the flounder. That's easier to remember. The chewier one is the rockfish.

—Why don't you call me Rockfish from now on? Because I'm so chewy.

Jesus, I'm losing it.

—No, I'll call you Flounder. Because I can see right through you.

The drunk man's slowing speech made him a little cuter. I listened to his cute, awkward talk as I ate more flounder or rockfish or whichever it was. I'd become very drunk very quickly and for some reason was thinking about Umma. She hadn't been allowed to eat anything raw since her cancer diagnosis six months ago, not even the hwe that she liked so much. Digging through the saury flesh that had come in the spicy stew, I had the uncharacteristically filial thought that I should bring her here when her treatment was over.

—Umma was always good at taking the bones out of fish for me . . .

Hearing this, he deftly ripped out the bones of his own saury and dropped the chunk of fish into my rice bowl.

—Oh no, I didn't mean it that way, please don't, I can't take your fish.

—I'm happy to.

—Me too. Saury is tasty.

—I'm not happy about the saury. I like the universe that is you.

Was this how the lovers of Pompeii felt when the magma covered them? I was deluged by something very hot, and the world seemed to stop turning. Spinoza had distinguished forty-eight different kinds of emotion. Which one was I feeling right then? Desire, joy, awe, or confusion? And what did the man on the other side of the table feel for me? A mix of disdain and curiosity, or something similar to what I felt for him? In an attempt to calm my pounding heart, I tried to recall the many keywords from the Philosophy of Emotions course but failed. In the blue light of the aquarium, he seemed paler than before. It was too late by the time it occurred to me that he looked lonelier than anyone I had ever known. His face grew larger and larger as it approached, and I was kissing him.

I tasted something on his lips that I had never tasted before. The fishy, chewy taste of rockfish. Maybe the taste of the universe.

That night, we both went back to his place.

◊

I lay down with him in the dark room and held him close.

I touched his hair, flattened from the cap he'd worn all day, felt his stiff neck and the tattooed skin that was cooler than the rest of his body. He put his arm around my shoulders. We lay still for a moment, holding onto each other without the least bit of distance between us. The shape of my chest, the length of my arms, my whole body seemed to exist in order to fit perfectly with his, and his warm head against my chest made me feel I was hugging something as vast and precious as a universe. Concentrating on the heat of his skin and the sound of his breathing whispering in my ear made me completely lose sense of who I was.

I became something not me, not anything, just another part of the world that was him.

◊

I remember what he said after we first had sex.

—Spinoza died of a lung disease.

—Did they mention that in class? Wasn't it tuberculosis or something?

—He was poor, he worked as a lens grinder, and the glass dust got into his lungs. He was an outsider among the academics. He couldn't get a teaching job, could only find manual labor, and that ended up killing him.

—How sad for him.

—That's why I'm doing this job. I've seen too many people ruined by their art or their convictions.

What could art have done to ruin anyone? And wasn't Spinoza a philosopher, not an artist? I didn't say any of this out loud. He kept talking in that overserious tone of his about things I had no interest in or didn't think important, but I pretended to listen. The air purifier by the bed toiled throughout his rambling. I stared at it as I spoke.

—I'm glad the air in here is so clean.

The semibasement apartment had blackout curtains, making it as dark as a cave. It was quite large, but crammed with so much stuff that I felt a bit claustrophobic. His giant desk was stacked with books by philosophers I'd never heard of, and he had air purifiers, dehumidifiers, and air conditioners in both of the two rooms. There was also an ergonomic armchair, a Scandinavian-style sofa and dining table set, and a rug that looked new.

—Your home is amazing. Lots of nice things . . .

—Actually, my umma was a Jasmine Black.

—What's that?

—It's a customer status department stores give to people who spend a lot of money. Like a VIP of shopping.

—Mm . . . OK. (*When was the last time I'd heard such transparent bragging?*) You must be pretty well-off.

—I used to be, but not anymore. I told you about it, right? That my umma is an alcoholic. She likes to shop when she's drunk. Look at how I have two air conditioners and dehumidifiers. The bookcase and sofa are all her drunk purchases.

—What a habit. Me shouting and kissing men when I'm drunk is nothing compared to that.

A joke, but it fell heavily into the dark silence that followed.

—My family went bankrupt because of it. I lived in an apartment in Apgujeong from the day I was born up to my college graduation, but now here I am in this dump.

What do I say to that? *Still, this isn't so bad, you're not about to die from cancer or anything, at least you got to live in Apgujeong at one point in your life,* were all not great options. Because I couldn't break my childhood conditioning, I began calculating his position on my mother's charts: an apartment of this size, grew up in Apgujeong, and a freelance editor.

The result? *I'm sorry, sir, we cannot offer you membership*. But I myself was a French graduate from a mid-tier university and unemployed, so we were the perfect leftover couple, and the feeling that even that was fated made me think I was well and truly dickmatized.

I fell asleep holding him in my arms, listening to him breathe. By the time I woke up, he was also beginning to stir. We both turned to face each other and looked into each other's eyes. I asked:

—Hyung, how did you know I was on "this side"?

—That was obvious the moment I laid eyes on you.

—Did you know we'd end up like this?

—Yes, from that first moment.

Who knew where this confidence came from? I was repulsed by this implied self-hating-gay dynamic, that he was the most masculine and attractive person on Earth and I was just some obviously gay super uber GAY GAY GAY in comparison, but I couldn't stop myself from falling headlong in love with him. To understand him, and beyond that, to understand my own thoughts and feelings as I crashed into him, and to interpret that whole mess of contradictions, I listened to every word he said, observed every little thing he did, and recorded it all. Desperately and plaintively, just like a grad student spending years writing their dissertation.

◊

That summer, I was totally obsessed. Obsessed and possessed.

He would invariably call after midnight, and I would leave Umma sleeping in her hospital room as I took a taxi to his place. The side effects from the Lasik surgery I'd had made the lights from the five hundred-odd streetlamps along Olympic Boulevard bleed into one another as the taxi zipped by, and the whole world looked like the inside of a dream. I paid the cab fare, about 15,000 won, got out, knocked on the steel gate of his building until I made the rusted hinges rattle, and finally there he was, a whole four inches taller than me, opening the door and emerging from the gate.

—You're here.

A shy voice. In the dim light his eyes were sunken and his lips protruded, so unbearably cute that even before I stepped through his front door I touched and stroked his face (he hated when I did that).

That night, we ordered spicy chicken feet and soju. We'd almost polished off three bottles of soju when he lay down with my leg as a pillow (unlike him, I was still a few shots short of the red-faced stage of drunkenness). He began to lay out his life history: He was born into a rich family in the Apgujeong neighborhood, but his father couldn't stand his alcoholic mother and deserted them early, while his older sister was married young to a Korean American and was now living in Virginia. He had lived with just his mother since university, until he put her in a hospital and moved out. The back of his head and neck grew warmer and warmer against my leg as he talked. I had a lot to talk about as well, being the caretaker of my sick mother and all. We both concluded that it was harder to handle their growing meanness and violence as they aged, and their extreme moods that seemed to shift by the second. He had been chattering on and on but suddenly fell silent; I looked down and found him asleep. What was he, a Kongsuni doll that went to sleep wherever you laid it down? His body spasmed a few times and he murmured, "Umma." A tear ran from one eye. *Well, this is a bit dramatic,* I thought; it was kind of funny that a grown man about to enter middle age was crying for his mother in his sleep. I stroked his head.

It was both awkward and nice that he kept talking about his family and childhood background. It was funny to see him get drunk on his own emotions and go into a serious actor-y mood when he talked about his family. While I was uncomfortable having to share my own family history as a kind of tit for tat, it was still nice to learn more about his life. I wanted to listen to him all night, for many nights on end. I wanted to fit together his fragmented pieces and complete the puzzle of him in my mind. The life that was unknown to me, the habits I wasn't aware of, even his breath—I wanted to reconfigure them all and make them my own.

Unaware of my obsessive thoughts, he slept blissfully until my leg started cramping, then his eyes jerked open as if someone had called out his name.

"You know you've been drooling, right?" I said as he got up.

Making the most adorably sheepish face, he wiped his mouth with his hand. He slowly got up and switched on the perfectly sculptured floor lamp (obviously another gift from his mother). The soft lighting fell on his back, and I could finally see the full shape of his tattoo. The pointed thing that reached the end of his finger was not a tail but a root. What ran up his arm and leg and stretched around his chest and back was a large tree. One that grew out of and covered a tiny planet, like in *The Little Prince*.

—Is that a baobab, like the one in *The Little Prince*?

—No. It's the Tree of Life.

—What's that?

—Nothing too meaningful. It contains the principle of the universe that I once studied.

He went on and on about how the universe was like a giant tree, some idea that combined sacred-tree myths from East and West, of invisible seasons and blah blah blah about death and rebirth, but all I could see from the tattoo was an attempt to cover up traces of an embarrassingly delinquent past with a more appropriately cool picture (not that the picture itself was either appropriate or cool). I could see through the thick branches and leaves some faint ghosts and red roses, lotus flowers, and dragons, which looked more like incomplete Irezumi tattoos.

—Didn't you just draw a tree over an Irezumi tattoo?

—Wow, you must have the second sight. How could you tell?

—Because . . . I have eyes . . .

A "hyung I know" (he had a hyung he knew in every social stratum, it seemed) who had come over from Japan when he was in high school had done the Irezumi tattoo for him. But this hyung was sent to prison before he could finish it, and the incomplete tattoo had only recently been drawn over.

—But do kids these days know about Irezumi? It was a fad in my day.

"A hyung I know," and "kids these days." His word choices really were like those of a stuffy, middle-aged ajussi. After a few more clues, I finally discovered that he was a whole Chinese zodiac cycle older than me—twelve years. Born 1976, year of the dragon, entering class of 1995 at K— University.

Despite the natural sense of a generation gap, it didn't change how I felt about him in the least. He stroked my short beard.

—Lying here with you in the dark . . .

—Yes, hyung?

—It's like we're the last two people on Earth.

—Oh, hyung. Enough with that.

Conversations with him at his house sometimes gave me the feeling that he was reciting lines from a Greek tragedy or an absurdist play, or even an eighties movie. Sure, it was partly because he liked to talk about existential stuff or his philosophy of the universe, but it was also because we spoke in formal Korean. I actually sort of liked it that way and thought it was a cute dynamic to have as a couple. What an idiot I was back then.

Around sunup, he and I would leave through the front gate that creaked as if it were crying. There was a dry cleaner in the neighborhood shopping center next door to his house. When the dry cleaner was open, he walked two steps behind me. When it was closed, he walked holding onto my little finger. I liked walking down the street with him hand in hand so much that I preferred to leave early with him. We would reach the main road together and stand shoulder to shoulder until the first bus arrived.

When the bus came and I climbed in, he would put one hand on my back then wave to me with the other. I would sit near the back and turn to the window, through which I could see him waving. The people around me would be dozing as I watched his form grow smaller and smaller. He would wave until the bus turned a corner and I vanished completely from his sight. He was the first person who had ever gazed after me that way.

For too long, I was caught up in the delusion that wherever I was and whatever I did, he would always be there behind me, waving. And so I would return to the hospital under the last remnants of moonlight, creep soundlessly through the newly scrubbed corridors, empty my bladder, and begin my day by listening to Umma complain about how bad her sleep had been.

◊

He and I continued to see each other after the twelve-week course at the institute had ended.

That small window of time, those few hours around dawn, decided the flow of my entire day. When we weren't together, I would wonder about where he was and what he was doing. I was always under his influence, whether I was half listening to Umma's complaints and taking care of her or making up stuff to put in my cover letters for job applications. Even while walking down streets I'd walked thousands of times before, I felt I was in thrall to his spell. Wanting to see the world from his elevation, I walked on my toes and looked out through what I imagined were his eyes. My thoughts were full of things he might be interested in or what we might do together as a couple. I felt my sensitivity to the world around me heightening with the effort.

That was probably why I went into that Gap store I normally would've walked past. There was a sign for a two-for-one sale on T-shirts. I got the same T-shirt in XXL and XL and put them in my bag. I might have even smiled, imagining the T-shirt hanging from his smooth, cold back.

That night at his house, I took out the T-shirts from my bag and presented them to him. His expression immediately turned cold, and he stared at the two shirts that were the same in design but different in size and color.

—I can't wear this.

—Oh. I guess wearing the same shirt might be a little too much. But maybe when we're alone at home . . .

—There's that, but it also has the American flag on it.

—What?

—Mr. Young, I do not wear clothes with this flag. Sometimes I think Mr. Young goes around wearing such symbols with no consideration of their meanings. Symbols such as the flags of warmongering countries. Do you really like America so much?

—Um, well, I mean, not really.

—Your music is all American.

—I like the divas. All gay guys do. What kind of a gay man isn't into Britney or Beyoncé?

—Who?

—Jesus . . .

But he was already on about how everything about America and the "American Empire" made him uncomfortable.

—The "American Empire"?

—Yes. American imperialism.

Imperialism. I had literally not heard the word spoken out loud since high school. What was there to say to that? His determined expression short-circuited my brain, and I felt nothing but the weird shame of having committed some obscure faux pas, with the American flag sewn on my shirt and cap. Not that I was ashamed of my supposed political ignorance (I've never been ashamed of anything like that). My shame stemmed from a fear that he would get sick of my ignorance and mindlessness and cut me out of his life. I was obsessed with getting him to like me, and I stood ready to change my entire value system for him. We spent our first sexless night after that. We didn't share a meal, our conversation was about nothing, and the distance between us refused to disappear.

The only similarity to before was his droning on until the sun rose about all the harm America had done to the rest of the world, how America controlled everything, from the world economy to global culture. He used words like "hegemony," "neoliberalism," and "cultural toadyism" like he was a social science textbook. But who cared about any of that crap? I just wanted to hold him, to fold every inch of my body and soul into his heat and heartbeat. Totally oblivious to such feelings, he brought his lecture to an end with this indictment:

—Mr. Young, you can't imagine what kind of world I've lived in.

As if you knew anything about my own world. Or even tried to. These words came up to my mouth, but I couldn't let them out. I had a feeling that they would kill what we had in an instant, that such words would only drive us further apart.

◊

While I was obsessing over him, Umma was obsessing over her own goal of achieving "complete remission" and using her characteristic diligence to achieve it. After a couple of surgeries, both big and small, she had become (in her own mind, at least) one of the foremost world authorities on cancer. She read every popular science book published on the subject, joined an Internet community that continuously uploaded the latest information on cancer treatment, and memorized the names and hospitals of every cancer specialist and their national rankings. It reminded me of how she had put together my college entrance strategy when I was a high school student, and of the devastation on her face when she saw my national college aptitude exam results. Just as she promptly gave up on me as soon as she saw my grades, my mother completely accepted the fact that she needed surgery once she heard that the cancer had metastasized to her lymph nodes. She said she would give up everything to the will of the Lord.

The Lord was in a whimsical mood, as this third operation, unlike the others before it, did not have a good outcome. Her biliary tract got blocked, and there was an infection in the surgical spot, which caused her temperature to rise up to 104 degrees. Her weight dropped to 99 pounds after she threw up everything she ate for two weeks. Taking care of her also made me lose weight, and with her vomit and diarrhea happening at ten-minute intervals, I came to the realization that life was merely the forward motion of going from one's first hospital room to one's last.

Being stuck with her all day gave me zero chance to meet up with him. I called once in a while, when I could, and even then it was mostly me listening to his metaphysical bullshit. During his series of weird stories, I conducted a psychological analysis of sorts as I listened, wondering if his propensity to ignore the problems of the real world stemmed from his feelings of helplessness in the face of his mother's daily drinking and subsequent shopping. I tried to learn from this by thinking: *You've got to grow up a bit in the face of suffering.*

Umma seemed to be feeling her physical pain in a different way than before. Unlike during her last recovery, she suffered from separation anxiety, and I had to be next to her always. She called for me as soon as she opened her eyes and didn't eat anything unless I fed it to her. I fed her, supported her at the toilet, cleaned up her vomit, and sat down on the caretaker's bed to write five thousand to ten thousand characters of an autobiographical novel.

We hired a private caretaker as soon as Umma was moved out of post-op to the regular ward. I would die before she did if I had to deal with her any longer, but more than that, I just wanted to touch him.

It was pure ecstasy to see him again after two weeks. There we were, six months after we'd met, seeing each other's faces in broad daylight on a crowded street for the first time. He looked a bit different when I saw him in the day. His dry skin looked even drier in the sun, and what I had taken to be the extended length of his eyes were actually deep wrinkles—that was the least of it. Out there among the people, he looked cowed somehow, and his head hung low like he'd been hit a few times.

He was trying not to show it, but I could tell he found it very uncomfortable to walk with me. I'd be lying if I said that didn't hurt my feelings, but I still felt passionate toward him. My hurt even turned into a kind of pity. Me at twenty-five, him at thirty-seven, our little fingers occasionally brushing against each other's but our eyes never meeting as we walked down the streets of Gangnam, stealing sideways glances and grins as we talked about nothing.

Just when I was totally soaked in the silly romance of our walk, someone called my name. It was a coworker from my previous company, the woman who ended up getting the permanent contract. I greeted her warmly (and in my mind cursed her for interrupting us). "How are you? I'm the same . . ." He stood a few steps away and scratched at the pavement with his foot. Glancing at him, my former coworker asked me who he was, and I just replied that he was an upperclassman from college. They awkwardly bowed their heads to each other, and we went our separate ways. *What kind of a thirty-seven-year-old still hangs out with a twenty-five-year-old underclassman?* she might have been thinking. My feelings about this were a bit complicated, but I snapped myself out of it. Life was complicated enough as it was. Why make it even more so?

And then there was that other time. As soon as the caretaker came to the ward, I took a taxi and went straight to Olympic Park. He was wearing his black hat and backpack as always, but the white shirtsleeves he had rolled up to his forearms and the sunscreen that gave his face a white tint made him look so cute I couldn't stand it. It was a weekday morning, and there weren't many people at Olympic Park.

When I thought no one was looking, I snuck a kiss on the back of his hand. He snatched his hand out of my grasp and said, "Don't do that," but he didn't seem to have disliked it. There was still an anxious atmosphere between us, which made us keep a six-inch distance from each other.

The cherry blossoms were in bloom, and white petals fell like snow whenever there was a breeze. The artificial reservoir was placidly still, the air was clear of pollution for once, the mood was calm, and there was an occasional young couple pushing a pram, or an old couple strolling hand in hand down the paths.

Stopping in front of a forsythia bush, he snapped off a twig of blossoms and slipped it into his buttonhole. This was somewhat shocking, the kind of old-man thing an elementary schooler's parent would do on Parents' Day.

—Uh, baby, excuse me, but what are you doing?

—I asked you not to call me that in public.

—I'd think what you're doing right now is a lot more embarrassing.

—And don't come up so close to me. Do you want to tell the whole world what we are?

—The entire universe knows what we are.

This offhand comment upset him so much that I ended up walking three steps behind him. Then he relented, came back to me, slipped the forsythia twig behind my ear, and took a photo of me on his iPhone. Pretending to want to look at the photo, I lunged at him instead, grabbing his waist, and this made him jump out of his skin. His reaction disappointed me, then seemed adorable, then annoying, my feelings shifting every second. But Olympic Park in the spring was so tear-inducingly beautiful that I wondered if these mood swings were because of the change in weather or because I was mentally exhausted from having looked after a patient for so long. These were my thoughts as I fooled around, propping blades of grass behind my ears and doing other silly things that couples do.

He suddenly stopped in his tracks. Someone was waving to him from a distance. A middle-aged couple so tightly arm in arm that one seemed to have placed the other under arrest. This four-legged wall approached us with alarming speed and greeted him warmly. He suddenly became very anxious, took off his hat, and bowed to them as I reflexively took a step back. They sounded like they had gone to college together. From a short distance, I shuffled my feet as I looked out at the end of the reservoir, enduring their incredibly boring conversation. A lot of blather about how someone from their student council days had been designated by a progressive party to stand for city council election somewhere, how someone else had written a political bestseller and was a panelist for a cable news show. We took up jogging as a couple and are reading Haruki Murakami, do you still like Nietzsche, what were you thinking when Park Geun-hye won the presidential election, darling, remember how I cried, who knew that such a terrible world would be possible in the 2010s after all we did as student activists, it was really beyond imagining . . . In any case, don't you meet up with your cohort anymore, look at you being all lazy. You were class president, it's up to you to set the tone for them. Darling, stop it, everyone is busy now. Yeah, kids these days have no discipline. Are you still with that publisher, the one that does theory books? I kept listening to their conversation/interrogation and saw how their torturous questions made his expression grow darker.

Suddenly, the male section of the middle-aged-couple-wall turned its head toward me.

—And who might this be?

—Oh, I'm just an underclassman.

—From school? Then you must be my underclassman as well. What year is your entering class?

—(*Why was this asshole, who just met me, using informal Korean?*) Not school, just from the neighborhood . . .

—I see. You live in Apgujeong in Gangnam?

—Uh, sure . . . (*Mind your own business.*)

—So how do you feel about Lee Myung-bak and Park Geun-hye?

—Look at my husband go. Please, pay no attention to him.

—Why? Isn't that something I can ask a young person? Tell me, do kids these days like Park Geun-hye?

—Well . . . She's kind of been around at this point.

—Kind of been around. What a refreshing perspective.

What about my perspective was so refreshing? Everyone in the world knew that Park Geun-hye was someone who had kind of been around. Why did these haggard oldsters, whenever they met someone young, namedrop a hundred people, spout tons of political views, and ask me what I thought? What would knowing what I thought change for them? Did they think that if we had similar thoughts and knew similar things, our differences in age would lessen? What were they going to do if I thought differently from them? Feel better about their ugly faces by proving to themselves how young and ignorant I was, how the years they'd lived hadn't been in vain?

The man seemed to detect my distaste, because he rudely tapped my shoulder and said, "You live in Gangnam, so you must like Park Geun-hye. I can understand it, you're rich." I bit my bottom lip. The wife said, "Don't be angry. He's just joking. We live in that expensive apartment block over there, ourselves." The two heads turned to each other and cackled as if she'd said something funny. I was just about ready to push this Great Wall of Smugness into the reservoir. Next to them, meanwhile, his face was growing as white as bread.

—But why are you out here at this hour? Shouldn't you be at work?

—Oh, I had some outside business.

He avoided eye contact in a way that didn't look suspicious at all. (He looked very suspicious.) The woman's eyes grew wide.

—Two men have business here? With all these flowers and the good weather?

—Oh, yes. It, it just happened that way.

—Then you must be lovers.

The man's joke made a smile break out on the woman's face, which she tried to cover with her free hand.

—Darling, you can't make jokes like that these days.

—Why not? The homosexual thing, the . . . queers? I'm not against it. I think it's possible they really exist.

—What are you talking about? Isn't it an evil colonial practice of the American Empire?

The couple clutched each other as they burst into laughter, and I thought, *What is this completely and utterly incomprehensible bullshit, the things these old-timers think are funny?* It was time to punch the eject button.

—We have to be going now.

—If you haven't eaten, why don't we have lunch together? I'll buy for your underclassman.

I answered over his obvious hesitation.

—No, thank you. We've already eaten.

—Already? It's only eleven.

—We had brunch.

Turning away from their shocked faces, I grabbed his arm and dragged him away. He complied, hastily saying goodbye. We were inside a taxi in a matter of moments.

His house was the most obvious place we could run away to. We needed to be where he felt safe. Because as annoyed at him as I was, I was worried. He looked absolutely awful. His hat came off as soon as we got inside. Then, he let out a deep sigh.

—Why did you have to do that?

—Do what?

—Why did you mention the word "brunch" to my upperclassmen? How do you think that makes me look to them?

—What do you mean, how does that make you look? It makes you their underclassman.

He was fuming, unable to let go of what had happened. I'd never seen him so angry, his emotions so intense. It threw me off. I could feel the thorns in my words as I spoke.

—Just who the hell do they think they are?

—My upperclassmen. They were student activists.

—They're nothing to you. Why do you care about what they think? Just lie to them and move on with your life.

—They're my upperclassmen.

The man had apparently been president of the student council, had been arrested protesting a few times, and was now some research professor at a historical organization. The woman, who had written short stories of their student activist days and received a prize given by a left-wing group, was currently a very important author. Being friends of friends, he worried that he would probably keep bumping into them in the future.

—Look, do you really have to care so much about what they think? So what if he used to be in the student council and she's a writer? They were being shitty to you and putting you down. Even I was annoyed about it. Why should you stand there and take that from them? Who cares about their opinions, who cares about what they think? Shouldn't you be grateful to me instead? We almost had to have lunch with them! And what kind of activists have such a horrible understanding of human rights? They're just a couple of champagne socialists—

—Don't . . .

—Don't what?

—Don't fucking talk about them like that.

That was the first time he had used informal Korean in my presence. It hurt enough to silence me. Without saying another word, I grabbed my bag and left his house. I hoped he would run after me. He didn't. I was more angry than sad, more despairing than angry. That was probably the first time he hadn't waved goodbye to me.

He gave me a call at dawn the next day. In a drunken voice, he demanded I come see him that minute. I dropped the formal language.

—I've got nothing to say to a fucking drunk.

—Language.

—Fuck your own language.

—When I say come, come.

—Fuck off. Am I your fucking dog?

—Please come.

I was his fucking dog. Off I trotted on my little puppy legs to his apartment, where I found him sitting on the floor on some spread-out newspapers, drinking soju with some banchan of octopus and rockfish. As soon as he saw me, he kissed me. The stench of alcohol made me push him away.

—Hey, stop that.

He said nothing as he silently started to take my clothes off and caress me. Looking down at his peach-like head and his face that looked like a dumpling gone cold, my resolve melted away, and I held him close.

After we had sex, he talked more about his past.

—My back isn't so good. I was incarcerated a few times.

—For drugs?

—No, for activism.

That was the day he went into his whole thing about being a student activist in his twenties. Smelling the odor of fish mixed with the soju on his breath, I curled up beside him as I listened to his voice.

He had been president of the humanities college student council. Now that I knew, it amazed me how the words "student council president" explained so much about him. The way he kept striding forward as if someone were after him, his constantly paranoid attitude, his tendency of letting others speak before saying one final thing as if he were the leader making a decision. He had been part of the leftover student activist generation of the mid-nineties and after graduation had briefly dipped his toes in the labor movement. The Misun-Hyosun incident demonstrations had also been during his time, as well as protests against the abolishment of the National Security Act and the anti–*Chosun Daily* movement, which caused him to be arrested a few times. His back and neck, he claimed, had never been the same since.

When he got down to the details, it turned out he had spent maybe seventy-two hours behind bars over four stays, he was never tortured, and all that happened there was some lying around in a cell with a heated floor. *A bit of a stretch to say you got a lifelong condition from that—maybe your back pain is just from bad posture?* These were the thoughts I didn't speak aloud.

The endless recounting of little incidents he experienced in the student movement made me feel drowsy and adrift. I listened to how he got a new tattoo every time he left lockup, and how he covered each tattoo whenever he had some new epiphany. Only half listening, I searched on my phone for information about the student council at his university and learned it had once been infamous for being hardline left-wing nationalist. I suppressed a smile at the eighties cliché of it all—listening to a former student council president reminisce about his activist days while we lay together in a basement apartment in the afterglow of sex.

—So I only use iPhones now. Not even the CIA can hack them.

His iPhone 4 looked tiny in his hand. He talked about how obsessive he was about security because he had been on the police blacklist during his peak activist years and his phone had been tapped and he himself followed. At that point in the story I thought, *What is this bullshit?* and realized he and I had never communicated through Korean messaging apps like KakaoTalk but only through iMessenger. Messaging apps with offshore servers, apparently, were safer.

—I'm anxious these days because I keep thinking someone is watching me.

I tried hard to keep a straight face.

—You still think there are people following you?

—Even at this very moment, there are people being wiretapped. And people who are killed for being activists.

—Well, yes. I know people are dying right this minute, people who are fighting for justice. I know that much.

It's just that I don't think you're one of those people. It's not that I don't believe you, or that I refuse to believe you, but I don't think you're that important a person. Today, you're just a run-of-the-mill guy sitting in his room all day and cursing out writers as you fix their spelling mistakes. You're as ordinary as I am. And what does that make me, who likes this loser so much?

I wanted to say all of these things, but I kissed him instead. Just so he couldn't say anything more.

◊

Olympic Park that fall was more beautiful than it had ever been.

Umma's cancer treatment was entering its final stages. To keep her strength up, she force-fed herself meals despite a complete lack of appetite. She also made herself go on walks. Despite all the food being stuffed into her mouth, her face became as gaunt as a skull. On a walk one day, she picked up a fallen leaf from the ground and said to me:

—I keep thinking of the time you were in high school.

—Jesus, now what?

—That time when you were sick. I don't know why I keep thinking about how I wasn't able to take care of you.

—I wasn't the one who was sick, you were. The person you weren't able to take care of was your own damn self.

Umma didn't seem to be listening and walked toward a flower patch instead. "Oh, look at this," she exclaimed, bent over a patch of decorative kale. They were shaped like ordinary kale, but their purple and red tint made them look almost alien.

—Ew, it looks weird. Umma, don't touch that.

—I used to really hate this plant.

—Why? You love anything that's a plant.

—This type of kale was the first thing I noticed after I failed to get into college. They were planted all along the street outside the school gates I'd walked out of after seeing my name wasn't on the acceptance lists that were posted. The purple color made me so nauseous, I had to hold down vomit. Such incredible disappointment. My whole life felt like it had ended back then, but look at me now, still alive.

—I'm impressed they even had kale back then.

—They did. They had everything we have now.

I thought about all the other things that had always been there as I supported her back to her hospital room.

◊

Around the end of that fall, I once met up with him when he came north of the Han River to hand over a manuscript edit he'd been working on. We fought a bit while drinking at a cheap pub near Hongik University when he commented that my inability to show restraint when it came to alcohol reminded him of someone—probably his umma. Tired of every topic of conversation being twisted back to his student activist days or his mother, I shot back that his inability to allow anything else but himself to be the center of attention was a sign of his having a mother complex. He retaliated by saying I had the same issue. Like any other accusation that wasn't completely wrong, the words left hurtful wounds, which in turn spiraled into a huge argument. The nice evening of drinking I had anticipated turned into a long fight in which we said things we shouldn't have said. Getting up from the bar with hurt feelings on both sides, we went out to the street to catch a cab. People were walking about with horrifically blood-splattered faces. Some were in superhero costumes and others were dressed as military officers. Halloween. *Damn it,* I thought. *It's bad enough that the night is ruined, it'll be murder trying to catch a taxi now.* He said, looking like he'd just eaten something rotten, that he was against Halloween because it was a holiday of the American Empire. He lectured on against accepting foreign customs without properly knowing what their origins were. I was so sick of him that I kept my mouth shut.

We were winding our way through the revelers, who were having much more fun than we were, when someone grabbed my arm. A zombie asked me if I could take a photo of him and his friends. Responding with a smile, I took a picture on his Polaroid camera of him posing with a Count Dracula and a Wonder Woman. He offered to take a photo of us as well and asked us to stand together. I slipped my arm under his and he stood there, stiff as a board. There we are to this day, awkwardly arm in arm. As soon as the photo was taken, he extracted his arm and took a step away from me. I asked him if he wanted the Polaroid they gave us, but he shook his head, hard. I slipped the little photo deep into my wallet.

That was the first and last photo we took together.

◊

The Tree of Life on his back seemed to wither that winter, and the Irezumi ghost underneath seemed to fade even more. I think it was because he was gaining weight. He had quit his usual thrice-weekly workout and taken on two more theory books to edit freelance. The wrinkles on his forehead deepened, and the smallest things set him off—the usual signs of someone going through a rough patch in life. Not that I was doing any better. I'd contracted chronic nasal inflammation, received text messages beginning with "We regret to inform you . . ." from the forty-eight companies I'd applied to, was sleeping only three to four hours at a time on the caretaker's bed at the hospital, and sat with my laptop on my knees punching out a story about a life that was and wasn't mine at the same time. There was no end in sight to any of this. No one would look at me in my state of constant exhaustion and take me for a twenty-something. Our daylight dates that had once been as exciting as spy missions were now gray and boring, and we had somehow reached a point in our relationship where everything about each other was just a part of the tedium of daily life.

We were watching a movie in his room while drinking soju and eating sweet-and-sour pork that we'd ordered in. On the flat-screen TV he'd bought there was an Eastern Bloc spy fighting for his life. I was bored with the slow-moving plot, but he watched in rapt concentration. At some point, I must've dozed off. The movie was over by the time I opened my eyes again. He was lying on the sofa, asleep. It had been a long time since I'd seen him splayed out like that, defenseless.

With nothing else to do, I sat down at his desk and turned on the computer. I killed some time looking things up on the Internet, searching his name and mine. I opened his bookmarks folder. There were all sorts of links to articles and blogs in there, seemingly stored at random. One article, from a pro–North Korean website, with the word "homosexuality" in the title caught my eye. Bored, I clicked on it.

> *Southern Korean society is facing increasingly complicated problems as time goes on. The foreign-worker problem, international marriage, prevalence of English language in employment and education, homosexuality and transgenderism, increase in studying abroad and immigrants, extreme individualism, too much religion, increased*

dependence on foreign capital, and the invasion of Western culture are problems we couldn't have imagined only a few years ago. ("The Path of the Nation," March 2007 issue)

What the hell? I thought, turning around to look at him. He lay on the bed facedown and naked, having kicked away the blanket. His back, as usual, looked like a child had drawn on it while he was asleep. His rhythmic snoring resounded through the room. I turned back to the computer and read through the bookmarked article. *"Southern" Korean society, foreign capital* . . . I paid special attention to these strange words. I couldn't understand them no matter how many times I read them. He'd used similar words with me before. Something sticky and vile, like slime, was engulfing me. Was this what he really thought of me?

I read through a few more pages in his browser bookmarks before closing the tab. All articles on the "disease" or "social ill" of homosexuality. I erased the browser history and turned off the monitor. Better to just carry on as if I had seen nothing. Especially since I was used to choosing to see nothing. I lay down next to him. The ruined graffiti of his back filled my field of vision. I traced my fingers over each line. They felt cold. Even after I covered us with the blanket that he'd kicked off, the chill did not go away. I curled up into myself with my back to him and suddenly felt that I was owed an apology. From whom?

The idiots who blamed homosexuality for every stupid thing? Or the specific idiot next to me for smothering himself in that bullshit and being unable to accept himself for what he was? Or the other idiot who fell for the first idiot, even when he knew the first idiot was an idiot, who fell for him so hard that he dug through his computer to know everything there was to possibly know about him? Maybe I was owed an apology from all of the above. Or maybe from none of them.

Maybe from Umma.

I really wanted a sincere apology from her. To hear her say, at least once in my life, that she was sorry. But that was never going to happen, was it? The thought that it would never happen turned my resentment into self-mockery for having thought such a thing in the first place, which then led me to think that I should just get my things and go. I got up, leaving him snoring on the bed. And for the first time ever, I left his house before daybreak. Like the decadent by-product of American imperialism and Western capitalism that I was.

◊

Around this time, I got a call from one of my old bosses from that company I'd worked at as an intern. Unlike me, running in place on the hamster wheel of life, she had moved ahead to lead her own division. They had just landed a North American contract worth ten billion won and needed workers desperately. While they could only sign people on with temp contracts, the workers could have their time count toward relevant work experience later if they went on to be hired permanently. We both knew this promise of a permanent contract was her dangling a nonexistent carrot, but things were dire enough for me to reach for it anyway. I kept bowing on the phone (as if she could see me), saying, "I'm your man."

On the day I got my first paycheck, I proposed that he and I take a walk to Chosun Hotel.

—A hotel? The two of us? Now?

—Not to sleep. Let's go to a nice restaurant there. Have some steak, some pasta.

—I'm not sure if I can afford that.

—Don't worry. My treat. To celebrate my new job.

He shook his head and said he didn't really like eating meat. Which was total garbage, because we'd been to about a million barbecue places together by then. He insisted he liked barbecue but didn't like steak. When I suggested pasta, he said we should get something like seafood stew instead. Or grilled clams, or seasoned crab.

—Jesus, hyung, do you like seafood that much? Were you a shark in a former life?

—It's just too strange.

—What is?

—Two men eating pasta at a restaurant.

And that's how our fight started.

—Do you think the world will split in two if two men happen to walk around together? What if, gasp, they were to even breathe the same air!

—While we're on this subject, I think you try to touch me a little too much when we're walking together.

—Oh, fuck off, no one is paying any attention to you on the street. Do you think you're still student council president or something? Enough with the diva complex!

—Do you know how obviously gay you are?

And that's how things got really nasty.

—Are you saying you're ashamed of me?

—Yes, that's right, I'm ashamed of you. You want to hold my hand in public, you call me baby. I mean, what would anyone think?

—Well, you know what, I'm ashamed of you, too, hyung. Your hideous, stupid trousers, your T-shirts with the stretched neck, your tattered backpack filled with all that crap—not even North Korean spies walk around in that kind of getup.

He stopped in the middle of the street. And for a while, he simply stood there. I simply stared at him standing there. Then, he turned his head and, without saying a word, walked away from me. *Who does he think he is?* I thought, and before I had the notion to go after him, he had already swiftly disappeared from view.

Had I made a mistake?

That was the first time I had seen him walk away from me.

Then, silence.

He stopped contacting me. No one picked up when I called. The phone indicated he had read my messages, but he never replied. This was the first time I had experienced such total and thorough radio silence from him. My lips dried out, and my heart seemed to shrink into itself with worry. I forgot about the rut we had fallen into. I again devoted every minute of my day to thinking about him: the first thing I thought when I opened my eyes in the morning was, *Is he going to call today?* and when I went to sleep with my phone under the pillow, all I dreamed of was him. There was only one question in my mind then.

Who was he, and what was I to him?

The longer I spent with him, the more I realized just how incompatible we were. It should have been obvious. He'd made it known from the start that he'd never wanted to accommodate me in any way, that he called me in the middle of the night when no one was around because he enjoyed fucking me and lecturing me afterward. He saw me as someone to teach and change, and I was unfortunately not receptive to that. There were many nights when I'd find myself unable to sleep, thinking of all this.

Then, after a week of silence, he texted me back.

How are you?

It almost made me mad at how easygoing he was being. Or to be honest, I was mad at myself for the burst of happiness I felt, but I couldn't help feeling that way. Tears came to my eyes. The more he seemed like a mysterious world I would never fully know, the more I wanted to conquer him. I wanted to squeeze him until he couldn't breathe. He didn't care if I was his, but I wanted him to feel that it was either me or nobody else. I wanted to grab his life by the balls and do with it whatever I pleased. So I made a huge, life-changing decision.

I would introduce him to my mother.

My suggestion was made in a light, casual way, as if it meant nothing to me, over a dinner of angler stew and soju. He was busily deboning the fish when I popped the question.

—Would you like to meet my mother?

He looked up with an expression of *Now what?*

—Why would I want to do that?

—I don't know . . . The weather is so fine these days. It would be nice to take a walk together in Olympic Park . . . I don't know.

His chopsticks searched for more angler flesh among the masses of bean sprouts in the big shared pot between us before giving up.

—All right. Let's.

—OK, hyung. Let's take a walk together on Sunday. And maybe have some coffee together.

—All right . . . I'll meet you at Olympic Park.

That was easier than I thought.

◊

As the date of her second operation approached, Umma made a big fuss about the nightmares she was having. *Look at her go,* I thought. She had always been so panicky when it came to work, her child, and her education. This was after her tumors had been removed, and the procedure coming up was only a simple one where inflamed tissue was being removed to aid blood flow. Someone would have to really try in order to mess it up. I thought this would be a good opportunity. The brief window that would open when the procedure was over, when she was about to begin her new second life, free from disease, filled with love for God and humanity and the universe . . .

That's when I would throw a bomb into her life.

For the sake of a future with Umma and him and me, for the life that remained for all of us ahead, I had to be brave. *Let's open the door and go outside. Yes, let's close our eyes and jump into the darkness.*

After accompanying my mother in the ambulance that transported her to Asan Hospital for her surgery, I went back to her hospice room to clean it up a bit. There was a photograph lying on her nightstand. The Polaroid of him and me.

I picked up the photo. My sloppy habits (and my old, stretched-out leather wallet) must've made me drop this photograph somewhere. Had my mother picked it up and put it on the nightstand, or had it been the caretaker? It surely was my mother. Who knows when I had dropped it, but to put a photo where I'm standing arm in arm with a man right where I would immediately see it, just on the day she was going into surgery, and then disappearing into the OR without a word—this was very much the kind of stunt my mother would pull.

She had always been that kind of person. Someone who knew everything, who saw through everything.

Even during the Asian financial crisis, when my father disappeared after bringing our household to ruin, Umma had seen through everything. "Son, we're going to go catch Father together." She and I got into her little red car and arrived at a rent-subsidized neighborhood in Incheon. There were so many spiderwebs in the stairways and corridors that we were flailing against them with our whole bodies by the time we pounded on the door of room 302. We knocked for a long time—I thought the apartment would shatter from the thumping—but there was no answer. After peering inside the window in the corridor for ages, trying to catch Father (and the Other Woman) in the act, we decided to return to the car. And just as we had turned the car around and were about to head home, we found Father in the empty lot behind the apartment building.

—Umma, look.

Father was playing badminton with a petite, middle-aged woman. They looked totally different from how I imagined them. There was something similar about the way they looked. Like two puzzle pieces, a perfect fit for each other. Father's face had an expression of calm that I had never seen during his whole life with Umma. An outsider who didn't understand the situation would've taken my mother and me for debt collectors come to make life hell for an innocent, ordinary couple. I will never forget Umma's face as she gazed upon the pair. That look she had, as if the whole world had stopped turning, surely could not be explained by any of Spinoza's forty-eight emotions. Its subtleties of feeling, brought on by that strange calm that Father and the Other Woman seemed to share, could not be simplified into concepts like despair or suffering. That feeling of pressing down on something that threatens to boil over or explode—it was the first time I learned of such emotions.

After her operation, Umma, despite the tubes of blood running out of her stomach, would get up from her bed at a certain hour and sit on the edge of it. She would light a candle on the nightstand, bring her hands together, and pray for over half an hour. Folding her stomach and legs like this could not be good for the recovery of her surgical wounds, but she insisted on repeatedly mortifying herself. After her prayer, she propped up the meal table of her hospital bed and copied verses from the Bible. Her obsessive transcription was like an ascetic practice. I suppose that instead of crying and screaming about her misfortune and ripping out her hair, she had chosen the method of copying out Bible verses, carefully pressing down the letters into the notebook with her ballpoint pen. That was the only penance that my mother, who had tried to refuse anesthesia, could achieve, and her transcription felt like a kind of breathing, almost.

A letter inhaling, a letter exhaling.

This act of breathing and writing struck me as being similar to the passion that ailed me at the time. Had it really been a passion for someone? Or a passion for the person I became when I was caught up in someone?

That was, in a way, a bottomless passion for me.

A passion for loving Jesus, for throwing oneself wholly into the act of living. That was, perhaps, the feeling I had toward my guy at one time, a feeling of giving myself up to something, an energy I was never a minute away from; perhaps it was something close to religion. To let oneself fall into complete darkness, a kind of faith.

I once discovered her sitting in this pose, unaware of her urinary catheter being dislodged. It made me so mad that I shouted at her. "What were you doing, do you think praying is going to change anything at all, how can you think this bullshit can help you in the slightest?"

Umma often used the word "miracle." That a fellow worshipper at church had transcribed the entire Bible in a thousand days and had been granted the miracle of healing. That she herself would also experience this miracle soon. The miracle hadn't happened to someone she knew personally but to the deacon's nephew's wife. For Christ's sake, the deacon's nephew's wife? Such a miracle seemed as unlikely as peace between Palestine and Israel. Umma added that she was not necessarily wishing for a miracle, she just wanted to have lived a life that the Lord considered beautiful. The only thing I could do was to call the nurse, against her stubborn refusals, to reinsert the catheter and change the sheets on her bed.

In those days of pain and disease, the only things she found meaningful were prayer and copying Bible verses. I'm sure this was how she truly felt. She did not look in the mirror or ever call anyone, she just wrote down letter after letter in diligent silence. I read this as her protest against my inability to stop my vice (namely, homosexuality), her resistance against this absurd cancer that had been inflicted upon her despite her lifelong diligence, her testimony of passion for life itself—all of these things mixed together in a kind of letter of complaint to the divine absolute. In the end, I could not talk to her about him, or about the photograph. I couldn't talk to her about anything at all.

◊

I couldn't get a hold of him on Sunday.

His phone was off and there was no answer to my text messages.

Umma and I took a walk by the reservoir, just the two of us.

I looked behind me several times. Of course he wasn't there.

Our walk that day was short.

◊

I got a text from him four days later. Something bad had happened to a hyung he was close to, and he couldn't pick up the phone. He said the word "sorry" like an afterthought, as if placing a sprig of parsley on a plate as a garnish.

Some hyung he had never mentioned before. Something bad happening.

Sure. That definitely happened. Something bad. And you were busy.

I didn't get angry at him. We carried on our conversation as if nothing had happened. Just like all the times before.

◊

Umma's cancer was declared to be in remission after a year and a half of treatment. Her doctor declared it a triumph of persistent and effective therapy based on state-of-the-art medical technology. I declared it a triumph of dedicated and selfless nursing on my part. Umma declared it a miracle sent to her directly from God.

Four days before she was discharged, he came for the first and last time to our house. I had decided to cook him a meal in our own kitchen since he found being together with me outside so uncomfortable. The prospect of a visit from him in broad daylight excited me. To watch him eat a meal I cooked with my own hands, in the place where I grew up! He arrived exactly on time, calmly laid down his backpack near the entrance, and daintily stepped into the house in incontrovertible "polite guest" mode, calling out the customary "Please excuse me." Glancing around the living room he added, "You have a lovely home." The first thing he did after this ceremony was to go straight into my room and look carefully at the spine of every one of my books on the shelf like he was an archivist at the National Library. He sat on my bed. What a sensation to see him sitting on my own bed! I felt so happy, I was walking on air. I took off my socks and crept toward him over my own duvet that had the scent of my own body, seeking a kiss from his lips. He turned his head slightly, pointed at the duvet, which happened to have a Michiko London duvet cover, and began to scold me.

—There's a Union Jack on this blanket.

—Uh, yeah.

—Mr. Young really loves the flags of Western countries.

—Not really. I didn't even notice that was there. You do know that you're the one obsessed with flags, right?

—There you go again. You always sound so defensive.

—I do not. I just talk the way I talk.

The mood chilled between us. I slid off the bed and said I'd make him lunch. Pasta, which I had never eaten with him, ever. In the kitchen, I cooked the spaghetti, chopped the garlic, heated a pan with olive oil, and sautéed the peperoncini and clams. I must say I was enamored by this image of myself cooking for him, seeing myself wiping the occasional bead of sweat from my forehead. It gave me joy that food I had made with my own hands would become part of his body. That satisfaction would be enough, I thought, as I plated the spaghetti and placed it on the table. He stirred at it with his chopsticks, not even trying to taste it. Then he put down his utensils and looked down at the baby photos of me underneath the glass top of our dinner table.

—Looking at these photos makes me think that your mother truly loves you.

—Really, now.

—Yes. There is something different about the face of someone who is loved. And something different about a photograph taken by someone who loves. And that's the thing, Mr. Young.

—What is, hyung?

—I think you should meet a good man someday.

— . . . What did you just say?

—Or maybe you should meet a good woman?

A thing as casually spoken as if he were suggesting we go for hwe instead of pasta. I couldn't reply to that. What else could I do but stare? Who would say such a thing as if it were nothing at all? Who was this man that I had obsessed over so much, this man I had been so ready to throw myself at? Suddenly the whole world had stopped making sense, and all I could do was keep staring. Did I, in that moment, resemble Umma as she'd stared at Father and the Other Woman playing badminton? Why so suddenly . . . or was it not so sudden? Had he found out that I had used his computer and dug through his secrets, that I had tried to turn his life upside down and see what I could shake out? Was it impossible to go back to the way we were?

He sighed and spoke again.

—What did you think we were? The two of us?

—What are you saying?

I grabbed his arm as he got up from his seat. I couldn't simply let him go like this—I wasn't Umma. I held onto him tighter as he tried to shake me off. He stared down at me with that pitying gaze of his, the one I was so used to.

—You didn't think this was *love,* did you?

I slapped him in the face, hard, before I could stop myself. By the time I regained my senses, I found myself with my hands strangling his neck as I held him down on the kitchen table, despite his being four inches taller than me. His face turned bright red as he struggled to get my hands off his neck. There were tears in his bloodshot eyes. The tears from my own eyes splashed his face and ran down his cheek. I let go. When I realized what I had done, it was too late, and after a few coughs, he got up from the table as if nothing had happened and put on his coat with his usual, sloth-like movements. Then he slung his ancient backpack on his shoulder and went out the front door, leaving me behind. I did not go after him. Instead, I went directly to the balcony as soon as he had left. I opened the window and stared out at his back. I stared and stared. I just knew this was the last I would ever see of him. I stared until he disappeared completely, until he became a dot that faded away, keeping him in my sight until the end.

A few days later, I rang the bell at the gate of his house. No one answered, no matter how many times I pressed. His gate, which once made a sound like a crying person as it opened, remained closed.

I left a letter in his letterbox. Well, not really a letter, just some ripped-out pages from the diary I had kept while we were together. Thirty pages overflowing with my emotions from the times I had spent with him. I didn't even recall what I'd written. Just like I didn't know what we had been, in the end. On the last page of my diary, I wrote that I hoped he would consider seeing me again, that I would wait for him to call me. I tossed it in his letterbox like throwing rubbish into a bin, this piece of my raw and still-beating heart.

Two weeks later came a text message.

Why don't you try becoming a writer?

There was no answer to my plea.

This bastard, to the bitter end, said only exactly what he wanted to say, never failing to condescend to me. All sorts of replies flitted through my head; I ended up putting my phone down. I made the decision, for the first and last time in our relationship, to choose what was best for me. Closing my eyes, I pressed Delete on his number. The digits came to mind as clearly as if they'd been branded down my cheek from my eyelid to my upper lip, but someday, I knew, even this would fade from memory.

In the end, we didn't even eat a plate of warm pasta together.

Instead, I drank pesticide. Pouring it into an iced Americano, I mused that to him even this coffee was a by-product of the American Empire (after all, it was called "Americano"), and a by-product of exploited third-world labor. That struck me as so hilarious that I was still laughing when my eyes finally closed. I shed no tears.

When I woke up again, I was in the ICU. Coincidentally, it was Asan Hospital, the same place Umma was at. My stomach had been pumped and doctors were administering hemodialysis; I could see Umma standing at a distance, watching. This was not the face I had wanted to see on the other side. The old Umma, when faced with this situation, would've screamed at me or hit me or burst into tears or started on a rant beginning "Dear Lord . . . " or acted in some other manner worthy of a melodramatic daytime soap opera, but that day Umma just stood there looking at me. And then she said:

—Don't try too hard. We all die someday, anyway.

I wanted to shout, *Why don't you give yourself that advice, aren't you supposed to ask me why I did it, isn't there something you always wondered about me?* I wanted to shout down the roof at her, but there was a respirator tube going down my throat, preventing me from speaking.

◊

For a while after that, it enraged me to hear people talking about love. Especially when it had to do with love between gay people; no matter who it was or what they said, I felt a violent, senseless urge to beat them up. *Our love is the same, our love is beautiful, our love is just another form of love between one human being and another . . .*

But is love truly beautiful?

To me, love is a thing you can't stop when you're caught up in it, a brief moment you can escape from only after it turns into the most hideous thing imaginable when you distance yourself from it. This is the uncomfortable truth about love that I learned in the ICU and recovery wards.

3.

Five whole years had passed since he and I went our separate ways. I was thirty and looked my age. I was a published writer, and I did not remember his phone number anymore. To tell the truth, I was too busy getting trampled on by life to remember a lot of the little things of daily existence.

It was Sunday again, and I was peeling some pesticide-free apples. A middle-aged woman sitting next to me, weighing in at ninety-nine pounds, was transcribing the words of Corinthians 3:2. When I offered her a slice, she refused by turning her head.

—You know I don't like apples. They turn my stomach sour.

—Stomachs are meant to be sour. Eat this so you can grow a new liver.

—When you're old, you can't grow back your liver so easily.

—OK, great. Why don't you be the doctor and the pastor and everyone else in the whole wide world?

Umma, her doctor, me, and everyone else in the whole wide world knew that she didn't have much time left. She said she didn't want an apple, she wanted to see the reservoir again. When I got up to get the wheelchair, she grew irritable and insisted she would walk on her own.

Ten minutes was all it took to get her exhausted. Her fierceness from just moments before had evaporated, and now here she was, bleating at me to find us a place to rest. We sat down, as always, at a bench near the reservoir. Umma breathed deeply and placed a hand on my leg. The many needles required for her treatment had made the veins on the back of her hand red. Her skin was like cardboard, like old leaves that would crumble when touched. She took out a note from her pocket and handed it to me.

Just as I care for you, the Lord also cares for you.

Jesus, Umma, you've sure got your priorities straight, why accept my pity when there's a chance to annoy me instead?

My eyes kept wandering around the reservoir. Whenever Umma stopped to catch her breath, I found myself taking a moment to glance around us, looking carefully at the faces of each passerby. It was so pathetic that I almost laughed at myself. I wondered what I would say if he did show up. Would I introduce him to Umma as if nothing had happened? Would I say I was glad to see him? Or would I ignore him and pass him by? Ridiculous to think that I could miss him. Any six-foot-four-inch giant standing around that lake was going to stick out like a sore thumb.

I had changed my phone number after I became a writer. There wasn't some big deal behind the decision—I just wanted my life to be a little different from the way it had been before I got published. A few clicks, and I had a new number. It would be a lie if I said I never thought of his number. It began with the numbers 010-81, but the other digits have long faded from memory. Still, I couldn't shake that feeling of having fought against something and lost. My hoping to forget his number in itself was just a forced, unnatural effort in the end. I didn't know what I truly wanted all this time, what I'd really been waiting for.

Umma and I sat down on the benches near the grass where the weird sculptures stood. It was the place where he and I were supposed to have met five years ago, the sculpture park. The more I tried to push him out of my mind, the more I kept thinking about him. He'd be standing there once I turned my head; I was sure of it. Why was I being such an idiot? Then I remembered the thick envelope in the backpack slung over my shoulder. The stack of pages didn't feel like paper but like something as heavy as a brick or a dumbbell.

I went through many men after I broke up with him. Love that disappeared like light rain over asphalt, hot love, urgent love that faded after a single night . . . I threw myself into all kinds of love, but I never fell for anyone as hard as I had fallen for him. There had been better men than him, much better according to every objective metric, but none of them really managed to gel for me. It was a long time after, a much longer time after, when I realized that he had taken the hottest parts of me, that in doing so he had changed me forever.

Umma suddenly got up from the bench and walked slowly up the hill. I followed her. At the top of it, she sat down on the grass. It was an early fall evening at Olympic Park. The fragrance of drying autumn leaves came right up to my nose. I threw off my bag and used my mother's emaciated thigh as a pillow. I felt like a nine-year-old again.

—Umma, why are you sitting on the bare grass? You used to tell me that sitting on the grass can cause viral hemorrhagic fever.

—When did I ever say such a thing?

—When I was ten. When you were getting your second online university degree. I remember you were wearing your graduation cap saying it. That if my bare skin touched the grass, I'd catch a disease where holes would appear all over my skin and I'd bleed from them. That it was from the germs in rat droppings.

—You're making this up. I would never say something so disgusting.

—You really said it. See, you can't remember any of this stuff. I remember everything. You gave me a lifelong phobia of grass because of it. To this day, I stick to the pavement and always avoid the grass.

—Really? How silly of me. The things I used to say to a child.

The sun began to set. Neither of us said anything for a moment as we watched it go down. Then, without taking her eyes off the sun, my mother spoke:

—Things are beautiful when they fade out.

—You think so?

—Son. Do you think I'm a very daring person?

—Why are you asking that all of a sudden?

—You know I've lived like a man for so long. I thought I feared nothing and didn't know anything about regret. But then I had you and realized that wasn't true. When you were a baby, holding you felt like clutching a fat purse, I felt so rich and satisfied. And it made me fearful. That you might get hurt, or break, or disappear.

—Jesus.

—One time when you were in kindergarten, I thought I'd lost you. Kindergarten hours were long over, but you didn't come home. The bus driver said you didn't get on the bus. You'd told him you were going to a friend's house instead. There was a panic. I ran out of the house and searched for you, all along the way from the kindergarten to our home until from a distance I saw your back. I decided to follow you and find out what you were doing. You kept taking a couple of steps and stopping. Looking into all the shops, every single one of them, observing and touching things. Your face full of curiosity. I wasn't angry. I was afraid. I realized that you weren't the child that I knew anymore. You were going to see what you wanted to see, walk where you wanted to walk and when you wanted to—you were a child with a world of your own. That filled me with such regret. Such fear.

—I guess I've always been easily distracted.

—I think that's why I was so terrible to you. I was scared. I wanted to keep you in my tiny soy-sauce dish of a world forever.

Umma grinned as she rubbed the part of her stomach where half of her liver, the source of courage according to folklore, had been removed. I hadn't seen her smile in a long time.

After her cancer came back, I kept dreaming that she would die.

In my dream, her car was no longer small and red but a big Volvo manufactured in the United States. The safest car in the world, they say. That wasn't the only thing different from reality. Umma didn't look like she was about to die; she was in her forties again, energetic and vivacious. In the dream, she drives the American-model Volvo straight off a cliff. It falls and shatters into a thousand pieces. Her hand sticks out from a window. The engine catches fire, beasts surround the burning wreckage like they're at a barbecue. Black smoke rises from inside the car, and something appears over her body. Decorative kale. It looks like blue fungus. It blooms and covers her in a flash, the scene of the accident suddenly obscured. And what are my thoughts as I stare down at all of this from the cliff? Do I cry? Laugh? Or feel nothing?

It would always be 5:00 a.m. when I woke up from this dream in a cold sweat. I would sit down at Umma's desk and begin to write, my back bent over the desktop that was pathetically small for someone my size. My sentences formed like lines coming out of my fingertips. They kept on coming without my thinking about them, as if they had a mind of their own. Then I would get a whiff of something burning, and the sentences that had driven on and on like a mad little red car would come to a halt.

Whenever I thought about what my writing meant to her, I felt as lost as if I was staring down the edge of a cliff. I was already thirty, a legal adult for ten years, and was old enough to know that my mother did not exist solely to hinder my existence but was a person in her own right who had fought hard making her way through life. She just happened to be unlucky. In other words, the fact that our relationship had been so terrible was as natural as cancer or fungus or the rotation of our planet or sunspots. I knew this, but the feeling that she was the source of all my problems kept nagging at me. I kicked myself for thinking this about a dying person, someone who was only skin and bones at this point, but the thought refused to leave my mind.

Me at ten years old terrified over bleeding to death from holes all over my body, me at nineteen writing about my mother to earn some extra cash, and me at thirty whipping myself up into a frenzy of vengeful hate to write stories about people who'd been kind to me, for strangers who didn't know me—all of these versions of me were sitting behind my mother that day.

Umma looked as hard and beautiful as ever as she gazed into the sunset. As I watched her, it suddenly occurred to me that she may indeed have read every one of my published stories and writings. Not that this would've changed anything, really.

She spoke in a sentimental voice.

—I used to feel that I'd been given the whole world when I held you.

Disease can turn anyone into a completely different person. Once upon a time, she'd been someone who was stronger than anyone else, who never looked back, who would rather die than say anything so sentimental, much less say such a thing as she looked into a sunset. It kept making me feel like I wanted to confess something, too.

—Umma . . . you know . . . there's something . . .

The words came before I could stop them, but I couldn't bear to say the words. There were so many things to say to her, and I wanted to say something, anything at all, but I hadn't a clue as to how to begin. *You know, Umma, there's something I wanted to say . . .*

I wish you would apologize to me for once in my life. About trampling on my heart that time. About giving birth to me this way, raising me this way, then deciding to push me away into a place I can't come back from, into a world of ignorance and being ignored, I wish you would apologize for that. I know that what happened to me wasn't really what you had wanted to happen, and I know it's not anyone's fault, I know that, but I—

—. . . I'll never understand it.

—Understand what?

—I'm really sorry, but I don't think I can ever forgive you for that. Ever.

—What is this child going on about?

I felt like I was about to cry. Quickly, I turned my head. I got up.

—Toilet.

I slung my bag over my shoulder and ran for the toilets. By the time my sanity returned, I found myself inside the wheelchair-accessible stall. I sat down on the toilet and took off my bag. I got out the stack of paper and held it in my hand. The twisted letters of my handwriting on the pages, his handwriting in red imposed over mine in black. I tore them in half, and in half again. I tore each separate piece into still smaller pieces and tossed them into the toilet bowl. The letters touched the water and dyed it red. When I flushed, the layer of paper on the water formed a swirl of confetti and disappeared down the hole.

I used to feel like I'd been given the whole world when I held him.

Like I was holding the whole universe.

Tears welled up but didn't spill over. There had been plenty of time to cry. I flushed repeatedly until the paper was all gone. Gathering my wits, I picked up my bag once more. I opened the door.

Umma was now lying on the grass and staring up at the sky. She looked incredibly calm. At peace. I wondered if that ninety-nine-pound, fifty-eight-year-old woman staring at the fading firmament was feeling the same way I was feeling. That my life could not be summed up like the neat columns of numbers on a chart, that it could swerve in an unpredictable direction at any time. That the person I thought I knew best just because we had blood ties could actually be the most mysterious and unknown. That there were times in life when you just have to stop holding on. And that was why the only thing I could do now was to cease all thinking, to simply watch her as she smiled and attached meanings to silly things like the rising and setting of the sun. All I could do was await her death. And hope that she would die without having known.

PART THREE
Love in the Big City

1.

Gyu-ho and I decided to go on a trip to Japan together, to commemorate our two-hundred-day anniversary. We pretended to be working in our respective offices while actually composing on a spreadsheet our itinerary for the three-night, four-day trip. Or to be more accurate, I would propose something, and Gyu-ho would automatically agree.

—We'll go to Asakusa, take pictures with the Doraemon at Odaiba, and do the hot springs in Hakone.

—Sure, sure.

We took so long packing on the day of the trip that we arrived with only minutes to spare at the airport. The queues at security and immigration made me sure we would miss the flight, but thankfully everything was moving fast. Until we presented two passports at the ticketing counter and one came back to us.

It was mine.

—Sir, this passport is expired.

Like an idiot, I had brought my expired passport, issued from before my military service. Gyu-ho was freaking out next to me ("What do we do what do we do") and we had only a few minutes until boarding.

I gave up and handed him the envelope of Japanese yen we had exchanged in advance.

—Pocket money from your hyung.

—What?

—Everything is booked and it's too late for refunds. At least one of us should get to enjoy it.

—You want me to go to Japan, by myself? What're you going on about?!

Gyu-ho's Jeju accent was rearing its cute head, which always happened when he was upset. I stuffed the envelope into his pocket and showed him the itinerary on my phone.

—Follow this plan and find some guy to spend the night with. They say Japanese men have bigger dicks. Have a million affairs. OK?

—Seriously, what the hell?

Gyu-ho grinned, more disconcerted than anything else, as I pushed him into the line for customs. He kept looking back at me, and I waved at him to go on.

I got back on the airport link alone. Gray, empty marshland stretched on and on outside the window. I felt like I was watching the same movie on repeat. My ears craved music, so I put on Kylie Minogue's album *Aphrodite* for old time's sake. Days like this reminded me of her voice. My lips kept drying out, but my pockets turned up empty—no lip balm. This was usually Gyu-ho's cue to hand me some of his. That wasn't all he did for me. He came home before me, cleaned the floor, had the stew cooked salty just the way I liked it, struck me speechless with the many ridiculous things he said . . . What was I going to do without him for four days? I thought of how long it had been since Gyu-ho and I had had sex. I'd never had a relationship so unmoored from sex before. And it was me who had told him to sleep around with Japanese guys, so why was I feeling shitty? Proving once again that no one is a bigger idiot than me.

◊

I first met Gyu-ho at what's now a defunct gay club in Itaewon.

It was Chuseok and they were having an all-you-can-drink tequila event. Not having a family to join for Chuseok—being a certified Unnatural focused on bringing shame to the family (not much has changed since then) and generally being stuck in poverty (yup, still)—I could hardly afford to pass up such an opportunity. I left the following message in our group chat:

Hey guys, there's an unlimited tequila event at G today. See you all there.

My friends were all in their twenties and would never say no to a free drink, and thus we "T-ara members" soon found ourselves strutting down Itaewon-ro in formation. I'd labeled our group chat after the girl group T-ara because there were six of us and I'm so very creative at naming things. I was the second shortest of the group and had a seriously nasal singing voice. Naturally that made me So-yeon, but that's not important; what's *really* important was that we had descended upon the club and were making our entrance.

Green lasers were flashing from the ceiling, as if they were frantically trying to take someone's eye out, and of course there were too many people at the main bar for us to get our drinks. The standing tables near the DJ booth were empty because the speakers nearby were so loud. We set up there. While the members of T-ara each had the heart of a delicate girl, we were mostly giants over five foot nine. We tried our darndest to go easy on the mincing and keep our shoulders wide and straight as we downed our tequila, our eyes rolling from side to side as we surreptitiously took in the scene. But soon, we were knocking it back: "Hey guys, slow down." "We're gonna get plastered." "Hey, Boram, you're already tilting. I said slow down." "Wait, where's Eun-jung gone?" "Ah, fuck it. Let's get drunk." So-yeon, whose liver was relatively healthy as he was in his twenties, overestimated his capacity a little too much and ended up dumping drinks down his throat like it was some overflowing sewer. And lo, the prophecy "We're gonna get plastered" came to pass.

That was when I noticed the bartender who was trying to keep up with the demand for shots. Shorn hair, cute guy. What did the neon letters hanging above his head say?

Don't be a drag. Just be a queen.

The speakers were pounding J.Lo and Pitbull's "On the Floor" directly onto our eardrums.

—Hey, DJ! Why the fuck do I have to listen to "On the Floor" at a fucking gay club?

Ji-yeon, the super-muscular guy with the prettiest face and shittiest temper of us all, went up to the DJ booth and screamed, in his amazingly loud voice, for him to put on some T-ara *right this minute*, but the DJ continued to look full of himself, pretending to be all serious with one side of his headphones held up to his ear. Didn't this pretentious fuck play the same old tired club mix every single week? *Look, asshole, is this America or Korea? Answer me. Answer me, goddamnit!* Ji-yeon was close to swiping the nerd's face with one of his paws. Boram and I each held onto one of Ji-yeon's arms, but he was a big girl at six feet and 185 pounds. Then suddenly, something flashed before my eyes, and when I came to, I heard T-ara screaming behind me. Or I heard them too late: Ji-yeon's elbow had busted my lip.

A face came right up to mine through the spinning stars and canaries. Very short hair, long eyes with uncreased lids. Hey, it's that bartender, no? I could see more of his pupils than the whites of his eyes, which made him look like an alien, and my face was reflected in them. I looked pathetic and numb and even a bit lonely.

But you, your sideburns curved into your beard, which tickled my face, you were so close. Something cold touched my cheek. A 500-milliliter bottle of Fiji water you had brought to my busted lip.

—Are you all right?

A deep, slightly hoarse voice. Lips with a hint of dryness covering a cute snaggletooth. It felt like a crime to let those friendly lips just pass me by. I kissed them before I could stop myself. Your tongue, which was as warm as your gaze, caressing mine—I wish that was how our love began, but this was long before it really started. I was just crazy. Over you? No, I was crazy from the excessive booze, the music, the chaotic laser beams, the stuffy air that felt like it could suffocate me any minute.

And more than anything else, I was crazy with my own piercing unhappiness.

I tasted blood. The taste shocked me sober and I pushed you away, then whispered in your ear.

—Please forget me.

I staggered as I got up from the floor. Yes, to tell you the truth now, after all that has happened since, I wasn't that drunk that night. It was just a stupid excuse in my attempt to gloss over the awkward moment. Boram and Qri shook my shoulders, and Kylie's "All the Lovers" started playing over the speakers. "Fuck this, come on, let's go." I pretended to be more drunk than I was as Eun-jung supported me on our way out of the club. Up on the surface, I magically sobered up and turned my head back toward the entrance leading down into the club. In the direction from which Kylie's voice continued to resound. The only thing I felt about you at the time was worry.

You, Gyu-ho, who tasted my blood.

◊

Kylie.

Summer of 2010, I went on my first leave from my compulsory military service, and the only three things floating around in my brain were iced Americano, Kylie Minogue, and sex. A man waved to me as I got off the express bus—K, my civil servant boyfriend of six months. He was holding a Starbucks venti extra-shot iced Americano in one hand, and I chugged that elixir of life so fast my eyes rolled up into the back of my head. Bitterness: my favorite taste in the world. That first coffee in three months made my heart pound like mad.

—Hyung, the new Kylie Minogue is out, I want to listen to it *now*.

—All right. Let's go inside somewhere.

We found a motel. As I threw off my uniform and showered, the hyung searched for the "All the Lovers" music video on the computer in our room, and I came out of the bathroom almost dripping wet to watch the hundreds of people take their clothes off, form a tower, and make the tower writhe in waves. We watched the mountains of naked people again and again, lay down on the bed, put on *Aphrodite*, and had sex. I was a little out of my mind because it had been a while, so when the hyung asked if he could do it with the condom off, I said yes. Around the fourth track, "Closer," he came inside me, and I went into the bathroom first to shower. We'd gone at it a little too hard—there was bleeding. Then it was back to the army after two nights and three days with him. Two weeks later I had a fever and red spots, and after spending a few days in the infirmary, wandering the border between life and death, I was sent to the military hospital.

The first thing the army doctor said to me when he looked up from my blood test results was:

—Are you a bottom or a top?

—Sir? I don't understand the question.

Apparently, that civil servant dogshit had fucked every man in sight as soon as I had entered bootcamp. I was returned to civilian status so fast my head spun, and the first thing I did to process my new reality was what I did best.

Creatively name things.

I named it Kylie, but not because my life had gone down the gutter while I'd been listening to Kylie Minogue. I just liked the name. If I was going to live with this thing for the rest of my life, I thought I might as well give it a pretty name, so Kylie it was.

Yeah. More than Madonna, Ariana, Britney, or Beyoncé, it's got to be Kylie. No question.

I've never regretted the name since.

◊

Even idiots who've drunk two hundred thousand shots of tequila the night before have to show up for work the next day. There I was, sitting behind a foldout table, trying not to puke. "Look at Me, I'm Sandra Dee." Sandy's whining was as uninspired as ever. The directing was a mess and the miscasting so irredeemable that the audience seats were practically empty despite all the comp tickets that had been handed out. I mean, look, no one was exactly asking for the ten millionth *Grease* revival. (Although this is coming from a guy who's fine with going to the same restaurant and same café for every date, as long as it's with a new man.) My only job in this graveyard was to stifle my yawns and catch what shuteye I could despite the horrendously loud music. Even in that dump, I occupied the bottommost pit. I wasn't in the cast, production team, or marketing, I was just the lowest of the low sitting glumly by the theater entrance, selling programs nobody wanted. In a whole month I must've sold just 400,000 won's worth, not even half my salary, which meant I'd be fired soon. What was this torture, sitting here on a Sunday night when all the normals were resting at home? Not to mention (to anyone) my running to the bathroom twice during the first act to throw up. My body itched to toss aside the programs and just go to bed, but Jaehee, my best friend from college, happened to be the one who got me this plum part-time job, and I couldn't let her down. The producer was some oppa she knew—I think they had slept together years before. Anyway, act 2 was about to begin, and what was that guy still loitering around the lobby for? I moved my ass, heavy as a planet though it was, over to where he sat.

—Sir, the intermission is . . .

The man looked up. Oh, wait a minute, this guy is familiar. That bartender from yesterday?

—Hey, you're the guy from the club last night, am I right?

—I think you are.

—Wow, coincidence! Are you here for the show?

—No. I'm here for you.

Damn. What's up with this guy? Does he like me? was what I could've thought, but I'm truly excellent at knowing my damn place in this world.

—Well . . . They won't let you in for the next fifteen minutes if you don't go in now.

He repeated that his only reason for being here was to see me. (Why, to sue me?)

—How did you know I'd even be here?

He'd seen a photo of the *Grease* tickets I'd given Ji-yeon on his Instagram.

#musical #grease #VIPticket #goodSeats #youngsGift

Of course. Another one of Ji-yeon's thirty thousand followers. I'd had strangers come up to me from time to time and strike up a conversation. Not because they were interested in me but because they wanted to talk to "Friend 3" of Ji-yeon, the gay influencer with the handsome face, ripped body, and big dick. You, bartender, must be trying to get in a good word through me. I wasn't a total idiot in that sense. But while we're on this topic, I should probably mention to you that I was nothing but a parasite feeding off his halo and waiting for scraps. I was the backdrop to my gorgeous friends, the big mama figure taking care of the drunk young'uns at the end of the night who couldn't flag down a cab. I didn't mind the role too much, but I was a little tired that day. I couldn't take care of anyone right then.

—Oh, too bad. It'll be a couple of hours before the second act ends and I finish cleaning up after. I don't think today is a good idea.

—That's fine. I'll just be on my phone at that Starbucks over there. Take your time.

He swept out of the theater before I could answer. I went back to my seat and fiddled around with the arrangement of the program booklets that didn't sell and wiped the spotless table over and over again with a wet wipe. But this was odd. Why was I smiling? Idiot.

The performance ended, the audience left, and I moved the life-size cardboard cutouts from the photo zone to the back and turned off the lights. It was after ten, surely he wasn't still waiting for me? Foolish of me to care either way, but I thought, *Why not see?* and went to Starbucks just in case.

You were sitting cross-legged on a sofa, your tortoiseshell-bespectacled eyes looking down at your phone as you played some game. That sincere expression you had beneath the dim club lighting was gone—who was this stupid-face? The spitting image of that cartoon penguin Pororo. You looked up and almost jumped off the couch getting to your feet and taking off your glasses, your face back to before. I couldn't hold back the laughter that burst out of me, and I was still laughing as I sat down across from you.

—Please stop laughing.

—Sorry. But why are you really here?

—You asked me to forget you and that made it even harder to do.

—Oh . . . Look, I'm sorry about the other night. I'll buy you a coffee. What would you like?

—I've already had some. Here, take this.

The thing he handed over was, Jesus, my white Louis Vuitton phone case. The most expensive gift that Civil Servant Dogshit had left me, from which I could still remember the feeling of the whole world turning into flashing neon lights when I first received it (a totally shattered memory now, but still, my one luxury-label possession), and I had dropped it?

—You were dancing so hard that you didn't even know you'd dropped your phone case. I picked it up for you.

— . . . Please forget Yesterday Me.

—Why? You were a great dancer. Especially during "Number Nine."

Fuck my life. I was already speaking two octaves lower in an attempt to sound more manly, but so much for all that.

As my face turned red from embarrassment, the Starbucks part-timer came over to where we sat and told us they were about to close, more or less booting us out the door. We walked without speaking along the alleys of Daehak-ro until I saw a sign for a beer place and blurted out before I could stop myself:

—Do you want to grab a beer?

This was not a clever move, as I was pretty resilient against most alcohol but not beer, but my whole life was basically a series of not-clever moves. I get stupidly honest when drunk, not to mention how I become a real dog, and of course that night I would start babbling on about shit no one asked me about. The worst was cataloguing the failures of my love life in what I'm sure was very attractive self-pity.

—Do you know what? I had true love once. I met an old man, twelve years older, a kind of activist, he made me feel bad about wearing American clothes. But I was the fool who loved him, bought gifts for him, cooked for him, rushed to his house so he could find me there waiting for him like his pet dog. But he dumped me. He iced me out. No regrets, though. Because it was true love. In any case, since then I've promised myself I will only meet nice guys. My next boyfriend was so-so in everything—face, body, dick, and whatnot—but he was nice, and that's why I went with him. Do you know why he dumped me? Apparently, I sing on the street too much. As if I was putting on a concert or something? Look, can't someone sing a song on the street if they want to? It's a free country . . .

The most pathetic highlight of the evening was when he walked me home, even though it was only ten minutes from the beer place.

—Do you want to come on up?

I saw him hesitating, and I suddenly came to my senses. *Get a fucking grip*, I thought. *He's just not that into you. Don't do this to someone who's just being nice.* I ignored how he kept looking around without saying a word and added:

—Where do you live?

—Incheon.

He came all the way here from Incheon? For a phone case? Because he was just being nice? This warranted further investigation.

—Haven't the trains stopped running? Stay until the first train.

—I can take a cab.

—Are you loaded?

—No.

—So you're so repulsed by me that you'd rather get in a cab to get away from me?

(How low was I willing to go tonight?)

—It's not that . . .

—Then what is it? Are you afraid I'll murder you? Eat you alive?

(Oh my God, please shut up.)

—I have this rule.

—What rule?

—To not . . . sleep with someone until the third date.

I burst out laughing. How old was this bastard, twenty? Had he seen too many episodes of *Sex and the City*, did he think he was Charlotte or something? It made me think he really wasn't that interested in me, but while I didn't want to make an even bigger fool of myself than I had up to that moment, I couldn't help grabbing his hand. I said one more thing that made my intentions transparently obvious.

—Did I say anything about sleeping? I'm just saying you can sit for a while and leave when the sun comes up.

He nodded. The complete mess that I lived in was laid bare as soon as I opened the front door, and that should've had the effect of sobering me up instantly. Except it didn't, I was still drunk, and so I tossed off my coat and pulled down my trousers, but why were my jeans so tight, had I gained weight? I ended up on the bed with my jeans only halfway down . . .

It was sunrise by the time I regained consciousness. As usual, this neighborhood, which was near a university, began its mornings with the construction-site clamor of new studio apartments. *Think of all the people who are going to be living in those rooms*. I frowned and opened my eyes. I lay on the bed in just my underwear and socks, alone. When I propped myself up on an elbow, I saw him lying on the floor, fully clothed. I got up and went to sit beside him. At the sight of his neat profile, the whole world fell silent. As if we were the only two people left in it. I wanted to lift my hand and touch his forehead, nose, and lips, but I was afraid of waking him.

Instead, I carefully brought my forefinger under his nose and felt his shallow breathing. His neck had accordioned into five wrinkles from using my big stuffed Pororo for a pillow, and he had laid his watch and wallet neatly on the floor by his head. I looked closely at his watch: "National Intelligence Service" was stamped on its face. What the hell? Curious, I carefully opened his wallet. Three thousand-won bills, a Shinhan Bank Patriots debit card, student ID for the You Sulhee Nursing Academy Juan branch, and a class 2 driver's license. Min Gyu-ho, born in 1989. He began to stir, and I quickly put down the wallet.

He opened his eyes, checked the time, and hastily began to put on his coat. He didn't drink the water I offered him as he stuffed his feet into his shoes. He was late for class, he said. It was only after, when he had closed the door behind him, that I realized we hadn't even exchanged phone numbers. Gyu-ho. Who wore a National Intelligence Service watch, worked at a gay bar, and was an aspiring nurse's aide.

I wondered what his deal was.

◊

Tuesday—the beginning of my week.

I had come back to university after I quit my first job. Mostly I rose late from bed and made a habit of sitting in the library, pretending to prepare for reentry into the workforce while actually just wasting time. In the beam of light coming in from the window next to me, I read novels, opened my laptop and banged out some crappy writing, or scribbled meaningless thoughts on notebook pages that were as blank as my brain.

Twenty-nine years old, You Sulhee Nursing Academy, nurse's aide, bartender, Min Gyu-ho.

I looked up from my meaningless stringing together of words at the light shining from the window. The drowsiness made me close my eyes for a bit, and when I woke up it was five in the afternoon. I dragged my body, heavier than its mass in wet rags, all the way to the theater on Daehak-ro. I turned on the lights in the hall and set up the life-size cardboard cut-outs of the actors next to the ticket office. In thirty minutes, I would be shouting "Programs for sale!" at the top of my lungs. Even when I knew that no one would want one.

I moved into a studio apartment with the excuse of concentrating on my job search (I couldn't stand living with my mother anymore). I took part-time jobs because I needed to pay rent and feed myself. And once I got a taste of what it meant to be in the real world, I immediately lost all appetite for building or achieving anything. *It's pointless—just the same thing in a different place,* I thought. *Frustration and rage, hope saddled with despair, the days dripping over you like sweat. It's the same thing with love. I'm too far gone to expect anything new. Looking for jobs, writing, men—all the same boredom. But weird how I keep wanting to write your name. You, Gyu-ho, who should be just another face among the many that populate these tedious days.*

◊

Jaehee called me while I was on my way home from a Saturday night performance. Her man was going on a business trip to Kuwait and she was free for the first time in a long while. She wanted to go drinking. I didn't really feel like it, but she said it would be her treat, so I took the bus to Hongdae with only my transportation card in my wallet. Jaehee had assembled a motley crew of people who mostly didn't know each other, who were out of school and in the real world, and out came the boring drinking games that real-world people played when they were with strangers, not to mention all that tedious shit about their lives that I had zero interest in, their yearly salaries, and their heterosexual dating stories. Bullshitting about who grabbed someone's hand or kissed or went out and had sex a month later. And what was with the Chungha instead of soju? The weak alcohol totally failed to get me drunk. "So anyway, when oppa was stationed at the Zaytun Division in Iraq, those American army bastards . . ." Some idiot who had gone to Korea University was making a huge fuss over his military service that literally no one had asked him about. I just kept knocking back glass after glass of Chungha, not saying anything.

—Hey, kid who keeps drinking, you still in college?

—No, I've graduated.

—Then you must be post-military. Where are you from?

I kept my mouth shut. Jaehee took the hint and tried to change the subject. "Look, oppa, no one is boring enough to talk about their military service days past thirty."

If boredom could be classified, tonight was truly world-class. While the others went on talking, I continued to chug down drinks and ripped the dried pollack in front of me into powder. I thought: *Damn, I'm so fucking bored. This is really not my thing.* This feeling of alienation that I was soaking in every day, every second of my life . . . *Hey, I wonder what the T-aras are doing?* I checked the group chat to see if anyone had said anything cute, but there was nothing new. Probably each had grabbed some guy to fuck or was sleeping off the week at home. I said I was going to the bathroom and messaged Jaehee from outside.

Sorry Jaehee. I'm leaving. It's too damn boring to stay.

Yeah, this asshole talks way too much lol everyone else hates him haha

Ok get the Korea University oppa drunk and have him pay for everything

You got it haha

I smiled as I stood by the curb. Four twenty in the morning. But you know what? I wanted to go somewhere, but not home. Only one place I could think of: Itaewon.

Like destiny, an orange cab slowed down in front of me. I climbed in and yelled, "Hey Mister, Itaewon Fire Station." Had the streetlamps and neon signs always been this spectacularly bright? Why was Seoul so beautiful all of a sudden? Everything that was once nothing seemed special and amazing somehow. And wouldn't you know it, the taxi fare still was more than 10,000 won, even when the surcharge period was over. Only

20,000 won left on this card, how was I going to get home later? Eh, whatever. I'd survive. The traffic began getting bad at Hannam-dong. I hopped out in front of the CJ Building and ran the rest of the way to G—. As I stood there, catching my breath, he came up out of the entrance, carrying a gigantic, full-to-bursting trash bag that was as big as he was. He didn't see me as he grunted with effort toward the parking lot where the bins were. I followed him. As soon as he dropped the bag, I hugged him from behind. I hadn't planned that part.

—Ah!

—Why are you so surprised?

—Ah *ssi, gaejjolahn*.

—Are you talking cutesy to me?

—My dialect pops out when I'm surprised.

—Incheon has a dialect?

—I'm not from Incheon.

—Then where?

—Jeju Island. It's only been a year since I came up on land.

Bwahahaha. "Came up on land"? It was rude of me, but I burst out laughing. His face read, *What did I say?* Look at that expression, all perturbed. Cute.

—Are you here with your friends?

—Nope. Alone. To see you.

—My God.

—You don't have to be so dramatic. I was drinking in Hongdae, but I could have another drink or three. The sun keeps trying to rise, I keep on thinking of drinks, and I kept wanting to come here. You guys mix a pretty strong drink, right?

He grinned and wrapped an arm around my shoulders. I was a little surprised at this sudden bodily contact but didn't let it show. I could feel his breath near my left ear. We walked like this to the club entrance, where the bouncer let us in with zero fuss, and he took me directly to the smaller bar. Then, he took out a double shot glass and filled it with a drink that was a color I hadn't seen before. I knocked back the whole thing: *Hell, it tastes like peaches, this isn't alcohol, it's fruit juice*. He poured me another glass. I'd asked him for a drink, not juice. But I slammed it back anyway.

Weird how I felt so much like dancing right then . . . the lights were bouncing off the forehead of his smiling face and it was strange how that felt like Seoul to me. Beautiful Seoul, loud music. Dark eyes, closely cropped hair. I wanted to dance with you and slide an arm around your waist and hold you against me. I wanted us to be close enough to feel each other's warmth. But why did my eyes keep closing? It was too hot and too smoky in there. My eyes were drying out. I wanted them to put on louder music. I wished they would turn on the mist machine. Anything to stop my eyes from closing . . .

When I woke, the fluorescent lights were on and all the clubgoers had disappeared. A few part-timers were left, cleaning up the unbelievably messy floor. Was this place really so small? The club with its lights on looked so different from the club at night, all tattered and dingy. And the most tattered and dingy thing about it, of course, was me. Me, sitting on a sofa in the corner. And there was Gyu-ho, sitting next to me.

—Sir, we're closing.

I bowed in apology to his smiling face and started to put on my coat, which had been put in my hands. Quickly making my way up the steps, I began to feel nauseous. Dear God, how much did I drink? It was proper daylight outside when I came out, one hand supporting me against the wall. A Paris Baguette part-timer was sweeping the street outside their storefront, and I sat down on the steps of the club entrance. My breath came out in puffs. But at least I hadn't fallen asleep on the street—it was so cold I would've died from exposure. Such a long way to the bus stop from here. I didn't have the strength to make it that far. I wet my dry lips and brushed the sleep out of my eyes as stragglers emerged from the club and scattered into the dawn. And here was Gyu-ho standing in front of me again, asking me why I wasn't on my way home.

—Uh, I'm sorry, but I haven't got the taxi fare?

And there we were, taking a taxi home together. Gyu-ho told the driver to take us not to Incheon but to the Daehak-ro district. The radio was playing Yang Hee-eun's ballad "Morning Dew." Gyu-ho spoke into the light music:

—Did you know this is our third time meeting each other?

—You were counting?

—I don't think you need to be counting to know that.

—Well, I was counting. Up to our third time.

Words disappeared. I swallowed, loud enough to be heard, and our knees were touching. I covered our legs with my coat. We held hands underneath it. Soon, we were stroking each other's thighs. Each looking in the opposite direction. We passed the Ambassador Hotel, Cheonggye Stream, and Ewha Wedding Hall, then the little theaters of Daehak-ro as we approached my house. Passing a firm and hot grip back and forth through our linked hands.

◊

We managed to keep the three-meeting rule once we were inside. Not that it was very successful.

Gyu-ho whispered, in informal Korean, "Can I take it off?" And I shook my head. Gyu-ho became shy.

—I'm sorry. It sometimes goes down if I wear one.

—(*A common excuse for those with erectile dysfunction.*) It's OK. Do you want me to do it?

—Well . . . I'm not so great at that.

◊

When I opened my eyes, I saw Gyu-ho standing in the kitchen. The rice cooker I hadn't used in at least half a year was on, and my soy sauce was out on the counter, along with all sorts of spices I didn't even know I had. Something was boiling on the stovetop. Staring into the slight steaminess of my studio apartment, I had the feeling of being in a dream. Gyu-ho, seeing I had woken up, told me he would make me breakfast in exchange for putting him up. I took out a low, foldable table from under the bed and wiped the dust with a wet wipe. No matter how much I wiped, there was still dust—how very much like everything else in my life. Gyu-ho, in the meantime, set down udon soup and some banchan I'd never seen before on the table. When I asked where the side dishes had come from, he said he'd bought them from the supermarket nearby. I suddenly noticed that there was a food-waste bag hanging by the sink and a bath mat I had never seen before in front of the bathroom. He was built for survival! Not even dandelion seeds could take root so quickly. I quietly ate up the soup he made me. It tasted of artificial seasoning. Gyu-ho said:

—You must've just moved here. No time to have gotten curtains.

—I moved here two years ago. I bought some curtains along with a bunch of sheets but they're stuffed away in some corner somewhere. I just couldn't be bothered to hang them.

—How could anyone live like . . . ? Wow.

—Can I ask you something too?

—Sure.

—If your hometown is in Jeju and you work in Itaewon, why do you live in Incheon?

He said it was because of his older brother. Just a year older than Gyu-ho, his brother, after four years of trying, had managed to get into a medical school that happened to be in Incheon. Around the time he was finishing up his premed courses, their mother came up to Incheon, saw how badly he was living, and sent Gyu-ho to help him out. Gyu-ho began to make his brother's meals, clean up his place, and be a companion (?) to him. I was surprised by this positively anachronistic, eighties-style narrative of the scrappy bumpkins who come up to Seoul for their schooling, but Gyu-ho seemed to have a different take on it.

—I was a troublemaker from an early age. I dropped out of high school. I even dropped out of the technical school I only scraped into. I felt bad for Umma, there was nothing to do on the island, and since I'm gay, I wanted to try living in Seoul. Not that Incheon is Seoul, but you know what I mean. So I came up.

—Isn't it hard living with your brother?

—It's hard. Very hard.

This spoiled brother of his seemed like a real piece of work. Saying he hated the rib stew Gyu-ho had cooked for him, he ate only the meat off the ribs and flushed the bones down the toilet, which remained broken to this day. When he was home, all he did was put on his headphones and curse loudly while he played video games. When Gyu-ho said they had barely exchanged ten words in their six months together, his face was shaded with an animosity that I had never seen in him before. Being the tactful-if-crafty little thing that I was, I changed the subject by asking Gyu-ho what he did during the week, to which he answered lightly that he went to nursing school.

—The government subsidizes it and they even pay you a stipend. I'm almost finished with the clinical part. Hey, do you know this song? *Let's go together to You Sulhee, You Sulhee Nursing Academy* . . .

The "song" was apparently the jingle to his nursing hagwon. I laughed and said I'd never heard of it; Gyu-ho looked sad and said that everyone in Incheon knew it.

—My parents said that when my brother sets up a clinic, I could get a job there helping him. Basically asking me to be his servant for the rest of my life.

He said this expressionlessly. What was he, a babbling brook? I could see right through him. And how did he know that complicated family histories were my special weakness? This was a punch I hadn't seen coming. In my not-so-short time living the gay life, Gyu-ho was the first person I'd met who put on no airs and was willing to reveal himself all the way down to the marrow. There was the look of someone who was stubborn as hell but managed to do everything he was told. He gave me the impression of being someone unusual in that regard. As I stared at him without saying anything, he looked back at me and said in a somewhat mournful voice:

—Really, everyone in Incheon knows it. You Sulhee.

I finished off the udon broth down to the bottom of the bowl and said:

—Are you busy today?

—Why?

—I can get you into a musical for free.

—Wow, really? Can you do that? I've never seen a musical before.

That the first musical of his life was going to be a production of what was said to be the worst casting of *Grease* in world history . . . I felt a bit bad for him, but what could you do? That's fate for you.

—I'll get you the best seat in the house. But I have one condition.

—What's that?

—I have a close friend named Ji-yeon. You know, that guy who hit me with his elbow?

—I know him. He's muscly and tan. Famous.

—Right. He can be an ass but he also has a knack for occasional insight, if you know what I mean. He said something to me once. That when two people are different ages but speak informal Korean to each other, they've had sex. So let's speak informal Korean.

—How old are you?

—I was born in eighty-eight, you in eighty-nine. You should call me "hyung."

—Hey, how did you know when I was born? But I'm an early eighty-nine. All my school friends are eighty-eight.

—This is the real world, who cares if you're an early eighty-nine? That's the way it is out here. Besides, you said you dropped out.

He said nothing.

—Sorry. I need to watch my mouth. But let's speak informally.

The pout of his thin lips provoked an urge to tease him with everything I had in my arsenal as well as a conflicting urge to give him everything in my heart, my world.

We walked side by side to the theater, where I got the guy in charge of ticketing to get Gyu-ho a seat. He went into the theater alone, and I sat down in the small glass case next to the box office as always, staring at the large monitor that showed the performance live onstage. Danny, in his tight blue jeans, got on the car and shouted:

—Greased lightning!

The little car on the stage would be shining its headlights on Gyu-ho's face. Was it weird that that small fact made me think Danny's unspeakably bad singing was a little better today? And there I was behind the glass showcase, humming, "Let's go together to You Sulhee, You Sulhee Nursing Academy." I was well and truly screwed.

◊

Gyu-ho barged into my house one Saturday afternoon. He took out a Bosch drill set from his gigantic backpack. He said he'd set his heart on purchasing it with the tips he'd collected from Chinese tourists over the Seol holidays, not that I could understand why anyone would set their heart on a drill set.

Gyu-ho took out the curtain rods and curtains I'd squirreled away in the corner of my closet. Then he started to put up the curtain rods, standing on a chair, while I held the chair steady and looked up at him.

—What is this obsession with you and curtains?

—You're always frowning when you sleep. It's kind of ugly.

I grinned. Gyu-ho got all sweaty as he installed the rods and hung the curtains. "I'm all done," he said as he came down from the chair, and I wiped his sweat. His warm forehead. The curtains, wrinkled from being stuffed in the corner for so long, really did block out even the tiniest ray of light. Like Gyu-ho and I were all alone in this world. He left the drill set by the desk and said he had to go to work.

—This early?

—Yeah. I'm having dinner with all the other hyungs.

—Aren't you going to take the drill?

—It's heavy. It's not like I'm going to use it anywhere else.

—(*Jesus, why buy it then?*) Sit down for a bit at least.

He was already late, he said, not pausing for even a glass of water as he whooshed out the door. I stared at the closed door. He came all this way to hang the curtains? From Incheon?

What the hell? So touching.

That night, I woke up to an urgent knocking on the door. Complete darkness. Fuck, who is this in the middle of the night? I picked up my phone: three missed phone calls, and the time was 7:30 a.m. Jesus, could morning really be this dark? I heard another series of knocks on the door and stumbled toward it, wearing nothing but underpants. There Gyu-ho stood with a box of macarons in his hand.

—Eating something sweet will make you feel better.

—What, are you drunk?

—No, we had our work dinner, but I didn't drink.

Uninvited, he shoved his way into the apartment, rubbing up against me, and popped a sky-blue macaron into my mouth. I chewed it. It was sweet, really sugary to me, and I don't like sweet things, which made my face, already scrunched from sleep, scrunch even harder.

Gyu-ho gently rubbed the frown on my forehead with his finger. I could smell the sweetness on his cold hands. He said:

—Do you want to go out?

—Are you crazy? I need more sleep.

—You've had plenty of sleep.

—What do you know?

—I've been calling you since midnight.

—(*The missed calls.*) What if I wasn't picking up?

—Please shut up and let's go.

Gyu-ho's pleading eyes and words were practically pushing me out the door. And I know I look like a stubborn ass, but I'm actually fairly sheeplike, being your standard Korean who managed to complete the state-mandated primary education curriculum and all. I took a deep breath, threw on a padded jacket over a tracksuit I normally wore as pajamas, and let myself be dragged by the hand outside, muttering all the way.

There weren't so many people out that early on a weekend, and we went along bantering back and forth:

—Where do you want to go?

—I don't know either, just so long as it's someplace not hot.

—It's the winter and it's not hot everywhere on the peninsula.

—I want to see more of Seoul.

—You're seeing it right now.

Then I suddenly thought of a place. Sliding my hands into the hood of Gyu-ho's padded jacket, I pushed him like a wheelbarrow up a slope. The scent of cigarettes wafted from his hair. In ten minutes, we were at Naksan Park. Gyu-ho's wide forehead was dewy with sweat. I teased him about him being too young to be out of breath over this little hill (even if we were just a year apart in age), then remembered he'd come here after a whole night of working, which made me feel bad for him. Not that I let him know that. Gyu-ho leaned on the old stone fortress wall.

—I wonder how old this gray stone is?

—Who knows?

Wordlessly, we stood against the ancient wall. I gazed out at the sun that was rising over the horizon, and it dawned on me that the earliest morning light brushed right up against the deepest hour of night. Gyu-ho stared down at Seoul as he spoke, not turning in my direction at all.

It was my dream to come up on land, to come to Seoul, ever since I was a child. I wanted to come to the highest place that I could come.

—There's Mount Halla right there in Jeju.

—You know . . .

—Yeah?

—Do you . . . want to go out?

—We're outside right now.

—Don't make me ask twice. You know exactly what I mean.

I know. I know, and that's exactly what I wanted to hear, and I do want to . . . The words came right up my throat . . . *but there's a situation that won't let me be with you. That no matter how much I want to, there's something I need to say to you first. Something I should have said from the beginning.*

I didn't know if I could say it, but I decided to go with my gut feeling.

—Gyu-ho, before we get serious, there are two things you need to know. The first is that I don't like sweet things. You don't need to buy me sweets like macarons. I'd rather have the money.

—Idiot.

—And there's another thing. Because, the thing is. The thing is.

◊

I've got Kylie.

Even though I'm known for fretting the small stuff and being the exact opposite over the big things, the first two months after being hit with Kylie made me lose my mind. I was medically discharged from the army and lying alone in my room, wondering if this really was my life now, if *this* was mine now. But you know, what more is there to it? There's medicine for it. I decided to pretend I was taking a vitamin every morning for the rest of my life. Sexwise, I just needed to put on a condom. Every person with any education or manners does those two things anyway. And I'd got to finish my national service in six months instead of other people's two years, so let's think of it as a lucky break. That was the extent of my thinking. I told my mother and the T-ara gang that I'd been discharged early for a ruptured disc. Because I had bad posture and did have a back problem, anyway. Apparently not all of them were total idiots because one of them did ask.

—What the fuck? Did you catch the bug?

—Oh no! You're on to me!

We cackled it away. When I drank with them, and some guy rumored to be poz passed by, our resident clown Eun-jung would say, "Everyone cover your glasses," and we'd all burst out laughing. I'd laugh along until I remembered, *Oh right, I've got it in me, too,* which sent a chill down my spine. But mostly I don't really think about it that much. I've had Kylie for five years, which means she's like family to me. Maybe even more family than family. We share the same blood vessels, partake of the same nourishment, draw the same breath—she is me, in other words. Another me. She'll be me until I die, even after I die. And she has to be mine alone . . .

—If you want to go out with me, you have to know this. That I am me, and I am Kylie as well. You're the first person I've ever had to tell this to. But don't let that pressure you. Not that I'm in a position to say this, seeing how I got to where I am by trusting a man too much, but I'm only telling you because I trust you for some weird reason. If you think this is too much, that's only natural, it's as natural as nature itself, it's all right if you leave now. Just keep it a secret for me. So I can keep having my life as it is now. Just remember me as some hairy guy living near Naksan Park. Or better, just forget all about me. Forget there was ever someone like me in your life and keep going to your You Sulhee Nursing Academy during the week and pouring drinks on the weekends.

Gyu-ho said nothing for a long time, seriously, not a single thing, moving not even an eyelash as he stared down at Seoul, and I paused briefly to think about what to say next before speaking again.

—OK, I'll get going. Go sightseeing for a bit and think about it and give me a call. Or not, if you don't want to bother. It's fine.

Pretending I really was fine, I followed the ancient wall back down into the city. The twisting, motion sickness–inducing path my feet were inefficiently walking me down made my legs feel strangely as if they were about to give way, and why was I biting my lips, my chin trembling? The walk was much farther than I'd thought. As I was thinking about just putting one foot in front of the other, a hand grabbed my shoulder. And when I turned my head, Gyu-ho was by my side, and his face, usually at eye-level, was a handspan above mine, since he was higher up on the path. From his small eyes fell large teardrops.

—How could you just say that like it's nothing?

—It really is nothing. Compared to all the other stuff life hits you with.

—Still . . . Why do you say it with a smile? It makes me sad.

—I should be the one crying.

There I was, staring at Gyu-ho as he cried. He was really ugly when he cried. Ugly but cute. Cute but pitiful. Funny that I was thinking he was the one who was pitiful. Gyu-ho swallowed his sobs as he spoke.

—You know, I like cats a lot. But I can't adopt one. I have allergies.

—Why are you talking about this?

—You look like a fat and mean cat. I'm going to call you Fatty Catty from now on.

Like "Kylie," kind of a weird nickname. But I still liked it.

◊

After a long time had gone by, on a night when we were lying in bed together, I asked Gyu-ho a question. Why, despite Kylie, did he decide to go out with me?

—Because, whatever it was or wasn't, you were you.

Because, whatever it was or wasn't—not because of it or despite it—I was me. I liked what he said so much I kept savoring it under my breath.

—Whatever it was or wasn't.

◊

When I announced that Gyu-ho and I were exclusive, the ones most overjoyed about it were the T-aras.

—Wow!

—Congratulations.

—Does this mean we enter the club for free?

—And do we get free drinks?

Can you believe those bitches?

2.

The first person between the two of us to get a proper job was Gyu-ho. Once he finished his clinical training, he immediately got several job offers at plastic surgery franchises and even at a urologist's clinic specializing in penis enlargement in the fancy Sinsa-dong neighborhood. A feat, considering how difficult it was to find work these days. Gyu-ho did have a reputation for being hardworking and resilient, but he was a little bit of a dunce in terms of planning out his life or making important decisions. Following my advice, he took the penis enlargement clinic job. And I turned out to be correct because he found out the work was easy and the pay high compared to the jobs taken by other people in his nursing school cohort.

The whole time we were together, Gyu-ho would ask me:

—Fatty Catty, what doing? Playing?

I surmised it was some form of Jeju dialect, cutting off the conjugations, which made me sigh and present him with the options most appropriate to his and our circumstances, like I was a mother bird digesting his food for him. I wasn't great at the daily stuff like cleaning the apartment or recycling, but I was pretty good at thinking through the big decisions. Of course, a monk can't shave his own head, as the saying goes, and my own pathfinding in life was a mess, getting rejected from a hundred companies I'd applied to and feeling like the whole world had turned its back on me. But all the same, I didn't really feel disappointed, let alone despairing, having experienced the universal truth that even if I'd managed to beat the odds and land somewhere, my life wouldn't improve that much anyway. And it went the same for relationships as well, giving me no swelling of the heart or great expectations when it came to our future together. And maybe that was the secret to our longevity.

Despite the drama of our beginnings, our actual relationship was perfectly mundane to the point of being yawn-inducing. But we didn't care. Because whatever it was or wasn't, we were in a relationship.

It became a habit of Gyu-ho's to come sleep at my place after his weekend shift at the club. He treaded softly because he knew I was a light sleeper and washed only his face before creeping under the covers and falling asleep in ten seconds. I woke, despite the faintness of the sounds he made, and nestled my nose up to the back of his head, where I could smell the tobacco in his hair or on his forehead as I tried to get back to sleep.

We'd get up late in the afternoon, boil ourselves some bean sprout or kimchi stew, and go out. I never would have ventured from the bed (especially not to go anywhere with crowds) unless someone told me to, while Gyu-ho felt caged in when he was in one place for too long. I couldn't understand how he had changed me, but thanks to him, I was now seeing the world.

The course of our dates followed the flow of Seoul's gentrification. The galleries of Samcheong-dong and Bukchon, Serosugil, near where Gyu-ho worked, and past Bogwang-dong, Mangwon-dong, Haebangchon, and Seongsu-dong . . . We each gained over ten pounds while we were together. Gyu-ho mostly picked up the check, for the sake of his minimum-wage, dirt-poor boyfriend. And whenever he told me to get famous soon and pay him back, I'd always answer with a boisterous "Of course!" But we both knew that was never going to happen.

◊

Gyu-ho came home one day with a piece of Australian beef to celebrate his promotion to Head of Consultations. What kind of two-bit operation must this clinic be to have given him a promotion already, I mused out loud as I cooked the beef. Hearing him talk about it, Head of Consultations didn't seem like it was that big a job, but the chief at the clinic did seem to have taken a liking to Gyu-ho. According to him, he was fond of Gyu-ho for not being like kids these days.

—What does he mean by me not being like kids these days?

—It means you're country as fuck.

I could tell what that doctor was thinking. Gyu-ho's frugality with words, his steadfast personality, combined with the looks of a juvenile delinquent—a combination that, oddly enough, inspired trust in his character. I should know, since that was exactly what attracted me to him as well.

Around the end of *Grease*'s run, I happened to stumble into a job at a medium-size shipping company. A company willing to pay me more than I was worth, to be honest, but there was one problem: the physical, the last formality in the hiring process. This being a relatively large corporation, they had subcontracted their physical exam to a hospital that could run full blood work panels. The university hospital doctor from whom I got my prescriptions assured me that it was illegal for them to test for the virus without my consent. But I couldn't quite take to heart what he was saying or shake off my sense of dread. Lo and behold, according to my Internet searches, someone had had his forthcoming employment contract at a major chaebol company canceled because of precisely what I was fearing. Seeing me worrying, Gyu-ho came up with a plan.

—I'll go instead. We have the same blood type.

In the beginning of our relationship he had asked for all sorts of stupid info like my blood type and astrological signs, saying he wanted to see if we were compatible—who knew that stuff would come in handy now? Not only did we have similar height and weight, but we were both type AB. Not to mention that people who didn't know us often had a hard time telling us apart (although I couldn't for the life of me understand why). A situation that was exacerbated when we both put on weight. Anyway, good for us, it was worth a shot. We decided to send him out instead of me. On the day of the exam, for which he took my citizens' registration ID with him, I was on pins and needles all day, worried that he'd do something stupid to blow his cover.

Easy as pie.

I sighed when I read his text message.

In the end, with two more performances to go before the curtains came down on *Grease*, I was able to enter the shipping company's training center. That *Grease* production, which had started with a triple-casting and shrunk to the two main principals with the narrowest vocal ranges, ended with over two hundred programs still unsold.

◊

Even after he got a nursing job, Gyu-ho did not quit bartending. His brother's vile personality was getting worse by the minute as he prepared for his licensing exams, and Gyu-ho was determined to move out as soon as he had saved enough for a rental deposit. Not only did he work five days a week at his day job, he did two nights at the club and even took a Saturday-morning shift at the clinic every other week. Our dates, which used to happen once or twice a week, shrank to once or twice a month. But at least he came to sleep at my place more often, collapsing into bed like he would never get up again. Now that we both had incomes, we could have meals at nicer places, and when we wanted to feel fancy we would book a room at a Seoul hotel. We'd drop a bath bomb into the tub, sit in the bubbles sipping champagne, never missing the opportunity to take selfies to upload on Instagram or Facebook, and then put on the hotel bathrobes and stare out at the city at night—all the usual things other people did. Of course, we didn't do the one most important thing. Or should I say, we couldn't? Gyu-ho would invariably, every single time, go limp as soon as he put on a condom, and if I became the one to put it on, he would bleed, and so we tried Viagra, but it gave us indigestion and blocked our noses. The panoply of medicine I had to take in the morning was already more than enough, including the digestive aids and liver protection pills. Moments like these were when Kylie, who was usually such a faint presence I could barely sense her, would suddenly appear and interfere with my life. But despite this, I decided to think of us as a completely ordinary couple of three years and not get all maudlin over it. Sometimes, I found Viagra generics or ejaculation delay medication in Gyu-ho's pockets. He said they were samples sent from pharmaceutical companies. *They're swimming in this kind of stuff.* Of course they were. But why was he carrying these things in his pocket? And I would think of the time Gyu-ho went to Japan alone. "Have lots of affairs, I'm fine." I was the one to say that. I had Kylie, and knew all too well that Gyu-ho didn't get to do everything he wanted to do because of her. I didn't want to be naive about it. I could keep Gyu-ho with me by not believing in anything. I could protect myself that way. It was all right. You can't have everything in life.

Kylie was my burden and mine alone.

◊

Gyu-ho, who'd said he had a rare day off during the week and was going to take a nap at home, showed up at my door completely incensed.

—What happened?

—I can't live with that bastard anymore.

That bastard who was his hyung, who only existed at that point to eat up the food Gyu-ho prepared, had begun to complain that Gyu-ho wasn't cooking enough because of his new job at the clinic. When Gyu-ho shot back at him, the bastard apparently opened the fridge and got out eggs to throw at him. I could feel my own face growing red with rage just hearing about it. There was still some yellow egg yolk on Gyu-ho's neck.

—Hey, let's call a truck.

And there went Gyu-ho and I, straight to Incheon together. It took two hours to get there by subway. To think he took this route both ways every day, for work and to come to my house. Thinking how we'd been together for seven hundred days but I'd never visited him at his place made me feel somewhat guilty. When we got out of the station and onto a bus, I heard an oddly familiar jingle playing on the radio: "Let's go together to You Sulhee, You Sulhee Nursing Academy, then it's off to nursing college, for you and me." Our eyes met and I tried not to laugh.

His bastard hyung was not home, he was probably off somewhere stuffing his face, and he hadn't cleaned up the smashed eggs in front of the fridge. I told Gyu-ho to pack his bag fast. He grabbed his clothes, two pairs of shoes, and a laptop. Everything fit into a large wheeled trunk.

—Is that it?

—Yeah. Plus the mattress I bought with my own money.

That was the extent of his share in that house. The moving truck that we had rented arrived just then, and Gyu-ho and I with our not-great backs managed to haul the super-single mattress onto the truck, groaning all the way.

Cold stars appeared in the skies that evening, and we crammed into the narrow passenger seat together in the truck, exchanging body heat through our thighs as we sped down the highway toward home. To a place that was no longer my apartment, but our apartment. The orange road lit up by streetlamps was making me tear up, and the city felt as if it were beginning anew.

Of course, that feeling did not last long. Try as we might, we couldn't figure out how to make Gyu-ho's mattress fit in my studio apartment. We ended up putting it in an awkward position by the sliding balcony doors, stepping on the mattress and pillows whenever we wanted to go out to the balcony. After four days of sleeping with me in my bed, Gyu-ho declared that my snoring was too loud and went to go to sleep on his own old mattress. Cold air seeped through the doors. Gyu-ho said that with the electric blanket on, his body would be warm but his nose cold, which he seemed to find hilarious.

Not long after he moved in, Gyu-ho quit bartending. He said he was feeling too tired to keep doing it, but I had a feeling it was because he no longer felt the need to work so hard for a rental deposit anymore. On his last night at work, the club owner gave him two bottles of Moët & Chandon. Gyu-ho's friends and mine gathered at a table to drink it up and celebrate.

3.

Once we started living together, we began to argue often. Not over anything big—just the usual stuff that comes from differences in lifestyles.

I considered drying laundry a life-or-death situation, which meant not only did I shake each piece of laundry several times before hanging it on the drying rack to prevent wrinkles, I also maintained a bit of space between each item, opened all the windows of the house, and even had a fan blowing on the clothes. As for Gyu-ho, he would randomly—I truly felt that "randomly" was the only word for it—toss the laundry on the rack and keep the windows shut so the house would end up like a sauna. These slow-drying clothes inevitably developed a sour smell. No matter how many times I nagged him, he never hung them properly, which is what compelled me to throw one of my T-shirts at his face after I got home from work.

—Look! Our clothes smell like rags!

—You're just smelling your own dirty face.

And the fight would progress until one of us was shouting . . .

Now that I was employed, I got into the bad habit of buying things to relieve stress. Gyu-ho was the same, and I tended to acquire books or trinkets while he competitively purchased clothes and daily essentials. Gyu-ho demanded I throw out books I wasn't going to read while I demanded he throw out clothes he wasn't going to wear. Neither of us was willing to compromise, and our small apartment was getting smaller by the day.

Gyu-ho couldn't stand how I let all my things just lie around the house. When he once said to me that everything should have its place, I retorted, "What place? Look at this tiny apartment! Wherever I am and wherever I go, there a place shall be, and that is God's truth." We almost broke up after the fight that ensued.

Even after hating him so much I felt like killing him, I'd find myself turning back to Gyu-ho as if nothing had happened and saying things like "What are we having for dinner tomorrow?" or "Please don't forget to buy trash bags tomorrow at the store." Mostly we slept on our own beds but occasionally in the same one, not having sex but taking turns giving each other an arm-pillow, breathing in the scent of each other's chests or armpits, slowly coming to believe that this was what it meant to love and be together.

◊

We coordinated our vacation days to visit Thailand together. The trip would be for a week, which was a long time for us.

Gyu-ho had kicked up a fuss making sure that I had my passport, that I wasn't forgetting anything. I would've told him to quit it with the nagging, but I couldn't in good conscience because of the bad precedent I'd set. Back when we were preparing for our failed Japan trip, we had gone together to apply for our passports at the Jongno district office. It was to be his first trip overseas, but he had acted like an expert; I did think that was a little cute. And this time, unlike the last trip we took, things went well for us from the beginning. We got a discount on our room at the new Park Hyatt in Bangkok because their remodeling wasn't finished. As a joke, we'd filled in "honeymoon" as the reason for our trip, but there was champagne and a card waiting for us when we got into the room. And not only that, the electric curtain was broken in the room we'd booked, which prompted the front desk to upgrade us to a suite on the top floor. As soon as we stepped into it, Gyu-ho and I couldn't help shouting out in amazement.

That night, we used some expensive Le Labo body cleanser to make a bubble bath, something we wouldn't do at home normally because of the price, and had champagne in the tub while making Marie Antoinette hairdos out of bubbles on each other's heads, giggling and taking photos. Drunk, we posted them on Instagram, finished the bottle, and lay in the tub until our fingertips wrinkled. Just as our bodies were turning red from the heat, we got out and put on our bathrobes and sprawled on the bed. I fell asleep gazing at Gyu-ho's reddened face.

When I woke from a dreamless sleep, I found us naked in each other's arms with our bathrobes sloughed off. There he lay in my arms, quiet as always. I touched the tip of his long nose and his cheeks. The air conditioner made them feel cold and dry to the touch.

We spent that morning shopping. Gyu-ho wanted to go to Khao San Road, which he'd heard so much about, and we decided to take a river taxi there. There was a squall as soon as we got onto the boat, and we were drenched through by the time we arrived. The rain kept coming down, and there was no place for us to go except a guesthouse nearby that charged around 50,000 won. After using the communal shower (basically a concrete floor with a few water hoses), we lay down on the creaking bed with our clothes off. And we had sex. Watching the ceiling fan rapidly slice up the air above us, I felt as if we had been connected into one body. I hadn't felt that way in a long time.

By the time the rain stopped, the sun was setting. We gazed at the atmospheric view and the violet sun as we downed a couple of beers. We bought matching Winnie the Pooh tank tops and put them on right away.

On Saturday, we wore the tank tops again, this time to the clubs. It was midnight when a familiar song started to play: T-ara's "Sexy Love." How many years had it been? A group of locals—my T-ara group's counterpart in Thailand—stormed the stage and began to flawlessly execute the choreography. Gyu-ho and I screamed as we hugged each other and hopped up and down. Gyu-ho's head felt warm and lovely, and we kissed right there in the middle of the club.

I've read somewhere that lovers will only quarrel when they visit Bangkok together, and we were the same. That one of us was staring after some guy, that the traffic was atrocious, and a whole score of other things I don't even remember squabbling about and getting into a wordless funk over—none of that mattered after a few pints and a kiss.

Because we were on vacation.

◊

After we came back to reality, we quickly became mired in the usual fatigue that came with the work we had to do for a living. The tank tops we wore in Thailand became loungewear. Pooh's face on the chest of our clothes started to pill, got splattered by broth from instant noodles, and then faded. Occasionally we laughed over our memories of the trip, but mostly we exchanged complaints about how dead tired we were, pinging them back and forth like we were playing table tennis. Gyu-ho and I had come to see each other as a part of a landscape of tedium. Just another prop in our monotonous, sweaty days.

After the trip, we began to argue more often than ever. Twice we even split up. One of the times we were apart, Gyu-ho moved out, and the other time, I did. We saw different people. A lot of people in my case, and probably the same for Gyu-ho. Once enough time passed and our hate, resentment, and reasons for fighting began to fade from memory, we got back together, moved back into the apartment, and asked no questions of each other as we silently made up and continued our relationship.

4.

After New Year's, we started taking Mandarin classes. Gyu-ho's hospital was planning to launch a consortium with a big Chinese medical corporation to set up hospitals in Beijing and Shanghai, which was what prompted me to suggest it.

There had been rumors circulating in my company that we were opening a China office too. And as the time we spent together had shrunk so much, it seemed to be a good idea to have something we could do jointly. On nights when classes finished late, we would take a cab back home together, staring off in opposite directions. Seoul's scenery passed by slowly outside the car window. The first time I met Gyu-ho, these streets were flooded with the light of neon. Thinking of my emotions back then, I couldn't help but grin. I had been the one to sign up for classes first, but Gyu-ho was making much better progress. I wasn't great at memorizing things, and unlike me, illiterate in Chinese characters from a young age, Gyu-ho used his characteristic diligence to forge ahead with great speed. He managed to obtain a level 5 on the HSK exam in only six months. I failed that level but applied for the post in Shanghai anyway.

Two weeks later, I heard the news that I and a coworker who had been hired two years before me were up for the post. Gyu-ho swiftly applied for his counterpart administrative position at his company's Shanghai clinic and got the job. They were even offering him a living stipend. We looked up where to live in Shanghai, where the city's gay clubs were, what the prices were like, and good places to buy furniture. While I was looking up the visa requirements for my job, I came across a clause saying that anyone wishing to reside for more than six months in China needed to pass a physical. A physical that included blood work. According to my search results, China was cracking down on sexually transmitted diseases that in recent years had been spreading among their population.

Kylie.

I had wanted too much. I'd already been given so much in the past three years. When you try to have too much, you're bound to stumble at some point.

The next day, I went to my boss and told him that due to my mother's illness, it was probably best for the company if I withdrew my application for the China posting. To Gyu-ho, I said that my coworker got the job. Gyu-ho replied that he would also stay, there were many hospitals that wanted him. As always, I gave Gyu-ho the right answer.

—You have to go. You can't just give up this great opportunity. You really should go.

Gyu-ho said nothing.

◊

And for two months after that, we lived the same way as before. We laughed at each other's jokes, kissed, deboned fish for each other and placed the flesh on each other's spoons, occasionally showered together, and in the midst of it all, Gyu-ho's new luggage set was delivered to our house and his things left our drawers and went into his suitcases. A flash, a moment of possibility—but I didn't go down that path. I knew the swelling of my heart would last only a moment. These feelings of aching possibility were only a sign that our time together was finally over for good.

On the last night we spent in the same house, I gazed at Gyu-ho's sleeping face. He slept like a dead man, just like always. Why did he never make a sound when he slept? Like he was afraid of being a nuisance to others. Like he was a burden, no matter how long we had lived together. Was that my fault or his fault, or just something neither of us could do anything about?

The next day, I went with Gyu-ho to the airport in Incheon. Once we checked his bags, we had about an hour left until his flight. Gyu-ho said he was hungry, so I went to a Paris Baguette to get the japchae fried pastry he liked and some milk. I shook my head when he asked me if I was hungry too. He was the one who was hungry, but he took only a bite of the pastry before asking me a question.

—Are you going to wait for me?

—They say going out with a local helps you pick up the language faster.

—Why do you keep smiling? Is this funny to you?

—You know I smile a lot.

—Are we breaking up?

—Stop asking me. No one cares anymore.

—And you don't care if we're not together anymore either, right?

Gyu-ho shoved the pastry he was eating into my hand. Then, looking like he was about to cry or was infuriated with me, he got up and walked swiftly toward the departure gates.

He was as big as a mountain, but he walked like an angry elementary school student. Rarely did he have such emotional outbursts—I suppose it was because I hadn't given him any of the answers he had wanted to hear. I sat there watching him disappear before turning my head.

The airport link was surprisingly empty, even for a weekday morning. Outside the window, gray mud flats and the dried-up tufts of harvested crops stretched endlessly into the distance. As I gazed out, I realized we were passing what was technically the city of Incheon. "Incheon is famous for You Sulhee." I mumbled the You Sulhee Nursing Academy jingle under my breath like a crazy person, and then looked around, embarrassed. I was the only person without any luggage. Just a half-eaten cold pastry in my hand. I looked down at his teeth marks in it. I had the urge to listen to a fun song, something by Kylie Minogue or T-ara, but my cell phone battery was drained. This was when Gyu-ho normally handed me a portable charger. And what else? He portioned out my pills and water every morning, passed me his lip balm when my lips were cracked, hung up blackout curtains in my room, scratched my back when it itched, took a shower first so the air in the bathroom was nice and warm. You were the only person who did those things for me, so honestly, Gyu-ho, I actually really care that we're not together anymore, a lot . . . I continued to gaze out at the scenery outside the window that kept blurring as the train sped toward Seoul, back to the big city that I knew so well.

PART FOUR

Late Rainy Season Vacation

1.

I was a little surprised when the Uber that Habibi had sent for me arrived at its destination, because what I'd assumed was a large shopping center turned out to be Bangkok's Park Hyatt Hotel.

I realized I'd forgotten all about the place once I stepped into the lobby.

The peach-colored palette of the lobby interior was just as it had been this time last year, the classy yet oddly cheap feeling of the twisted chandeliers, and the chestnut-colored carpeting that muffled each footstep. The French man who introduced himself as the proprietor stood in the same place wearing the same clothes, which made me smile. This was exactly the same building as before, but looking back, I was standing there feeling utterly different.

The proprietor called me Mr. Park and held out his hand. This unexpected hospitality brought another awkward smile to my face. His French-accented English. His name card slipped inside my passport. When he asked how the friend I'd come with before was doing, I just kept smiling. And simply said, as clearly as possible, with no awkwardness in my manner or voice, the room number on the thirtieth floor and Habibi's name.

When the doors to his room opened before me, I was surprised again not only because Habibi seemed more tired and older than when I had first met him, but also because the layout of the suite was so familiar. Sometimes, the memory of a space can come to us faster than that of a person or a scene. Half-opened motorized drapes, fabric sofas that smelled new, a bathroom laid with black marble. The same as the suite I had stayed in a year ago.

Habibi put his hand on my shoulder and we embraced. I didn't know much about him. A financier who had studied economics at an American university. Thirty-nine on Tinder, but much older in reality. He wore formal attire, even a necktie pin and cufflinks, a Rolex watch, and had various currencies in a Louis Vuitton wallet. The only other thing I knew about him was the fact that at the end of October, late into vacation season when I had nothing special to do, he had called.

But it wasn't as if I had realized that much about myself, either. Just a few months ago, I never would've thought that I would, at thirty-two, be going on a late-rainy-season vacation at the end of October.

◊

After Gyu-ho left, the first thing I did was throw out his mattress.

Until not long ago, there was a super-single mattress and a queen-size Tempur bed lying side by side in my tiny studio apartment. There were also two bookshelves and a desk, as well as a refrigerator, leaving almost no room to move about. Gyu-ho had brought the super-single mattress when he moved in, the same brand that not long ago made the news for having carcinogenic compounds in its materials; I recognized the Taegeuk-style logo underneath. I kept thinking of Gyu-ho complaining about how his back hurt the longer he slept, which made me smile. The Tempur bed had been gifted to me by my father, when I was first published in a literary magazine, because I had a bad back. Father had expanded his business despite the bad economy and was going around with a wallet stuffed with so many checks he couldn't close it—while nonetheless giving off all kinds of ominous vibes. And of course, not even a year later, he'd been accused of evading taxes and embezzling funds through a dual contract and was currently on the run.

There was a stain somewhere on the mattress from soy sauce we'd spilled on it.

As I hauled that radon-spewing mattress out on my own, I thought back to the time Gyu-ho and I had sushi together on it. Something good must've happened that day. Sushi was celebration takeout.

One time, while sitting on the bed eating his sushi, Gyu-ho (always clumsy) flipped over his plate by accident, and I quickly wiped it with my sleeve. A brief moment, but a stain remained on the mattress.

By the time I realized my back wasn't sound enough for me to haul out a super-single mattress on my own, it was too late; I felt jolts of electricity all the way to the ends of my toes as I just barely made it to the complex's recycling area. When I got back to the room, there was a report on the news saying the company responsible for the carcinogenic mattresses was offering to pick them up and dispose of them for free. The pain in my back throbbed, stubborn and persistent. It was too late to put things back the way they'd been.

◊

The second thing I did after breaking up with Gyu-ho was quit my job.

I had been reassigned to the administrative support team around the time Gyu-ho left. "Administrative support" was a fancy term for procuring toilet paper, mops, highlighters, and other office junk to distribute within the company. A job any elementary school student with decent math skills could do, and it was the perfect work for a person like me, who had no special skills or ambition. The company was satisfied, and I should've been satisfied too, but every day I was caught up in an inexplicable, silent rage, and every morning I begged the gods that I would not ruin yet another day being mired in vicious resentment. In the new office, I gradually turned into a hairy Sasquatch that made no effort whatsoever to be sociable, and just slouched around, hoping no one noticed me. I had said the same thing to myself in the last company I'd worked for, but I kept my mind intact by vowing over and over that this was the last time I would take on a corporate job. Soon, my thirty-two-inch waist ballooned to thirty-six inches, I got promoted to middle manager, and I reached the point where I had to shop at specialized online stores for big and tall men. My body and heart grew heavier by the day.

After Gyu-ho left, it became difficult to get out of bed in the morning. I was occasionally late for work. Sometimes I forgot to wash my face or shave—I even walked around all day with my zipper down or shirt buttons unaligned, only realizing it when I got back home. Routine hygiene tasks like shaving, clipping my nails, and brushing my teeth were starting to feel like lofty luxuries. As much as I may have looked like some hairy thug off the streets, I had actually never ever been absent during my twelve years of primary school and was slightly obsessive about showering before going out, which made these developments a new experience. I started taking home things from my desk at work. Soon after all my personal items were gone, I handed in my notice. I did not feel excited or hopeful or relieved. Just tired of everything.

◊

The third thing I did after splitting up with Gyu-ho was get on a plane to Bangkok.

If I had followed my initial plan, I would've lived an extremely enlightened and elegant life. Sleep from midnight to eight, make pourover coffees at home, exercise for three hours a day, learn the guitar, read all the books I wanted to, write, shop thriftily . . . But when I opened my eyes in the morning, I hadn't a clue what time it was or whether the sun was even up. My circadian rhythms were completely shot. If, at first, I felt guilty about wasting my life away, I soon came to think, *Well, whatever. Let's see how far my money goes, let's go as far as life will take me.* And lying there on my Tempur bed, I came to the realization, *Wow, this really is a very plush and perfect state of death, even boredom can get boring,* and turned on my phone to do some half-hearted swiping on Tinder. Anyone would do, anyone to get me out of that coffin of a bed and into the world outside, from the rotting cesspool of my life to what lay beyond. I racked up swipes like I was repopulating the Earth. And when I got a match, I messaged, *Where are you now?* And finally dragged myself from bed to have bad sex for the sake of going outside.

I'd matched with him by pure mistake, back in Seoul.

A body in a suit, thirty-nine years of age. I found it so hilarious that he made a point of saying he'd majored in economics at Columbia University that I tapped his profile for more. To see what kind of an idiot went to such great lengths to hide his face and identity but proclaimed where he went to school—an Ivy League university, at that. The idiot turned out to be "Alex," a Malay Singaporean. His favorite book was Keynes's *Employment, Interest and Money*. His favorite artists were Bach and Rachmaninoff? Of course they were. He must have traveled a lot for business, because his profile came with a long list of dates of availability per city, and he was in Seoul for only a few days. Looking through this silly profile, my thumb accidentally hit Super Like. We matched, and he immediately messaged me. Could I come to his hotel? I thought for three seconds and replied yes, I could. He gave me his room number at the Four Seasons. Not bothering to shower, I put on my tracksuit that I wore for pajamas, pressed down a cap on my head, and headed for the hotel. The receptionist gave me a suspicious look as I came in, and I knocked on Alex's door with no hopes of any sort for this encounter. Because life had always been eager to fail my expectations, no matter how low I set them.

As I showered in his room, I thought, *It's been four days.* It was funny to me that your scalp could get so itchy that it hurt.

Sex with him was neither good nor bad. The lights were down low, the room was bigger than I thought, and I could smell Tom Ford's Leather on his neck. All I could think of was that my face felt dry since I'd applied nothing after coming out of the shower.

While he was in the shower, I looked through his Louis Vuitton wallet and took a photo of his ID, just in case. He was in his mid-forties and his name was Habibi. Of course his name was fake. Chinese money, Hong Kong dollars, Thai baht, and some unidentifiable denominations. His job must have involved a lot of travel. There were some 50,000-won bills, and I thought for a second of taking a couple but didn't. I don't know what came over me to even think that in that moment.

He came out with a bath towel around his waist. I'd done nothing wrong—well, I hadn't stolen any money—but felt weirdly guilty and avoided his gaze. I was practically curled into myself like some cornered wild animal when he looked down at me and asked me a question.

—What does *jeuk pay ching sai* mean?

—What? What's that?

—I hear it outside the hotel. Protestors shouting it.

—Uh . . . *jeok-pye-cheong-san*?

—Yes. I think that's it.

I burst out laughing, much to my own embarrassment. I laughed until my belly ached, until realizing it had been a long time since I'd laughed so hard. If ever . . . When was the last time?

—Is it something funny?

—No, it's just . . .

Jeok-pye-cheong-san. "Get rid of old, evil practices." I didn't know how to explain it in English, so I fell silent. An awkward pause.

Habibi looked as if he were thinking something over before asking me another question.

—Do you want to go to Bangkok together?

◊

The room I had booked with Gyu-ho had been a king.

The Park Hyatt at the time was in the last stages of remodeling and not all of the facilities were operational when we got there. Needless to say, there weren't many people staying. Gyu-ho invariably got into a panic when it came to making choices, which is why I ended up choosing our flights, hotel, and even the length of our stay. Of the 1.58 million-won hotel bill, I paid 780,000 won and Gyu-ho 800,000. It was a splurge. I knew I was burning money when I confirmed the reservation, but I adamantly believed it was worth the sacrifice. We were desperate for rest and relaxation.

As soon as we got to the twenty-first floor, we tossed our backpacks on the floor and fell side by side onto the bed, our shoes still on. Gyu-ho stretched out an arm and gently rubbed out the frown between my eyes with his hand, and I stuck out my tongue to lick it. His unwashed hand had a hint of salt. Lying on the bed, we stared out the windows that surrounded us. There was a clear view of the grounds of someone's grand house below, so grand and well kept that it looked more like a theme park than someone's house. After staring at it for ages, I was desperate for a quick nap and so took off my shoes and clothes. Gyu-ho dug his nose into my chest, and I could smell a familiar scent in his hair. I probably smelled the same way. I pressed the button for the curtains to close. The light slowly dimmed. About to close my eyes, I noticed that the curtains hadn't closed completely, and light was streaming through about a palm's width of space.

—You have got to be kidding me.

—Let's just sleep.

—No, look. The curtain won't close completely.

—Sleep, damn it.

—How can you sleep with this light streaming in?

As I called the front desk to tell them the curtain was broken, Gyu-ho covered his face in the pillow and mumbled, "Here we go again." A handyman came up to our room, checked the curtain, and called up the concierge to take a look as well. He was a middle-aged Frenchman in a suit. The concierge politely informed us that because the hotel was still in its preopening stage, there were some kinks to be worked out, and they would upgrade our room. When I passed on this information to Gyu-ho, he smiled his usual weary smile. The concierge slung our backpacks one on each shoulder. His sleek suit and our ragged backpacks looked oddly good together. We followed him down the corridors like two giant hamsters. And the room he ended up putting our backpacks down in happened to be right below the penthouse. As he handed us the keys, he said my family name, Park, and pointed out that we were in the Park King Suite, which made Gyu-ho pipe up that the name of the suite sounded like an RPG boss that was tough to defeat. As an additional gesture of apology for the inconvenience, the concierge invited us to a party being held at the rooftop bar at nine, adding that drinks were free. I did my Very Fancy Person impression and said that we would endeavor to make it. But as soon as the doors closed behind the concierge, Gyu-ho and I hugged each other and screamed. The room was vast and luxurious beyond what we ever could have imagined.

I took out our passports and Thai baht from Gyu-ho's backpack. The passport covers had Pororo characters on them. I sometimes called Gyu-ho Pororo, since his eyes also shrank when he put on his big glasses. Meanwhile, I had a big face and prominent nostrils, which was why my passport cover was of the dinosaur Crong. I put our Pororo and Crong passports and money into the black-cloth-lined security box.

When Gyu-ho and I went to the Jongno district office, he hesitated over deciding how to spell his name in English. I wrote down "Q-ho" for him instead. It made him glad that the spelling was easy to remember. I whispered in his ear:

—It stands for "Queer Homo."

—Do you want to die?

Gyu-ho was surprisingly bad at English but was great at East Asian languages like Mandarin or Japanese. I was the complete opposite of him and once got the lowest score on a Chinese character test in high school, an exam I had actually put a lot of effort into studying for. The teacher told the whole school about my result, a humiliation I carried with me for a long time. But I'd watched so many episodes of *Friends, Will and Grace,* and *Sex and the City* on repeat that my English was all right.

That evening, we spent a ridiculous amount of time choosing outfits for each other. The clothes in our backpacks were mostly shorts that doubled as swim trunks and cheap 6,000-won T-shirts from H&M, and we tried to find the least cheap-looking things we'd brought with us. Collars added a modicum of formality, so we ended up going with matching polo shirts, jeans, and sneakers, as not to show our wriggling toes.

The elevator took us to the thirtieth floor. I practically had to block my nose and pop my ears.

When the elevator doors opened, we were greeted by a party in full swing. Flawlessly pomaded men with pocket squares tucked into the breast pockets of their sharp suits, women with off-the-shoulder gowns and thick makeup . . . A DJ of indeterminate race was playing EDM beats. Cartier bracelets and Patek Philippe watches, Van Cleef & Arpels necklaces and Hermès shoes were drifting past us as we stood there, taking it all in. A hotel worker came up to us and took down our room number, told us it was a standing party, and encouraged us to enjoy ourselves at any spot on the roof. Gyu-ho went up to the DJ booth, which was almost two stories tall, and reverently examined the woofers and amps before I finally managed to drag him to a seat with a view of the city. We sat on a slippery leather sofa, our shoulders touching, and stared out at downtown Bangkok. I picked up a cocktail menu that had no prices listed and ordered a "motorcycle." It was rimmed with a salty-sweet spice, which I licked off with my tongue, and which helped the alcohol go down easily—this great drink was free? We got a little too excited as we ordered everything on the drink menu, and the whiskey-based cocktails got us drunk fast. One drink tasted like grass, another was sweet, another bitter, another . . . Soon it didn't matter what we were drinking, we simply looked at each other's burning-red faces, touched our hot foreheads, licked the spices on the rims of our glasses, and kept drinking. As if we were going back to when we were children with ice cream. The sight of it was so funny, we kept laughing. Everyone else was laughing, too, not just us, and the drunker we got, the better things felt, and we held each other in the balmy night breeze, taking in the blurring Bangkok night lights, happy like we were five-year-olds again.

2.

After I broke up with Gyu-ho, I published a short story collection.

I'd been writing throughout my time with Gyu-ho. There I was every day, coming home determined to get some writing done, tossing off my socks before sitting my butt down in front of the computer. Gyu-ho would come back from his Chinese classes, pick up my crumpled socks and put them into the hamper, and sigh. There he was, holding out something sweet to eat to my irritated face. He always said nothing worked better to calm my nerves than something sugary. Then he would sit down on the bed with the stuffed Doraemon doll and say to it:

—My, my, my, what a grand artist we get to live with, am I right?

—You've ruined my day's work.

I would complain as I lay down in bed next to him. His little finger rubbing away the frown between my eyebrows. The smell of water on his hand. I bit his finger, and Gyu-ho pretended it hurt. (Or maybe it actually did.) Whenever I failed to write what I'd wanted to write, or despaired that there were so many things in this world that seemed within reach but really weren't, Gyu-ho bought me takeout dinners of Japanese curry or fried rice.

—Why aren't you eating?

—Uh, Gyu-ho.

—Yeah?

—I . . . hate curry.

Gyu-ho died several times in my short stories.

He drank pesticide, hung himself, was run over, slit his wrists . . .

Gyu-ho became a straight man, a gay man, a woman, a child, a soldier . . . He became anything and everything a human being could possibly become before dying on the page, every time.

And as a dead person, he became the object of my love, my reminiscences, my dreams—always an object. In my memories, Gyu-ho is cold, perfectly frozen in time.

That is how my memories of him are preserved under glass, safe and pristine, forever apart from me.

◊

Sometimes it feels as if everything was all my fault, and sometimes I think: *it's all so unfair.*

That was the first thing I thought when I woke up in the morning. It was followed by all sorts of illogical, extemporaneous thoughts swirling up and consuming my time on this Earth. Was it before or after Gyu-ho had left me when these unwanted thoughts began to deluge me in my quiet moments? My watch said it was past noon. No longer the morning, in other words.

The night before, I'd gone to that same rooftop bar with Habibi. It was completely open this time, with a higher level that had been closed off before, and so we sat down at a table underneath the stars and shared a bottle of champagne. This time, I'd come prepared with a button-down shirt and a pair of linen trousers. I requested a blanket because of the chill.

Habibi grinned at how I didn't let a blanket around my shoulders make me put down my champagne flute. I couldn't help grinning at him either, as our different backgrounds and ages left us with very little in common. I asked him about his life in the United States. (Elites love talking about that stuff, I've learned.) Habibi's reply was shorter than I expected.

—It was brutal. And I was lonely.

—Really?

For that reason, he explained, he had ended up finishing his bachelor's in three years and immediately found a job at a multinational investment bank. (He said it in that humble-bragging way that elites have.)

—Repressing my emotions while working in that bank gave me ulcers, headaches, and insomnia. Then the darkness came.

—What?

—Darkness. Literal darkness. My vision kept blacking out. The hospital said they could find nothing wrong with me. I spent two weeks alone at home. Once the lights had gone out in my life, I realized I knew nothing about myself, not a single thing. What I liked, what my room looked like, how I had lived so far, what I was supposed to do on a break, what I had to do to get the lights back on . . . This was the first time I didn't have a clear and set path in life—I felt completely powerless.

—I see.

I could sympathize with him. Overwork and stress. I knew what they could do to someone. But this blackout situation seemed a little overdramatic, and I didn't like the direction the conversation was going; I switched tracks to something lighter.

—Did you meet any guys there?

He smiled and nodded.

—Well, my name does mean "love" in Arabic.

He was about to say something more but then appeared to think better of it and threw back his champagne instead. Had he met an Arab man? Curly hair and long eyelashes came to mind. And was this guy CIA or something? Why couldn't he give a straight answer to anything? Clamming up every time my curiosity was piqued. Not that he seemed to have some big deal of a story. His voice cut through my thoughts.

—Does your name have a meaning? I think Koreans all have meanings to their names.

—"Shine brightly from somewhere high." My father paid actual money for that name.

—Like a star?

—Like a nuclear weapon.

Even at this stupid joke, Habibi giggled. His face looked so tired in the dim starlight. I had a sudden urge to console him (most uncharacteristic of me), but I reached the reasonable conclusion that I was just feeling self-pity. Drunk, we got back on the elevator, and I stared at a spot of pomade on the back of his hair as I followed him to the room.

◊

I woke up to the sound of something cracking in the bathroom. What the hell? Drunker than I had realized, I saw that I'd fallen asleep in my clothes. I walked to the bathroom, swaying a little. The sliding door opened to reveal Habibi collapsed by the toilet. I wasn't sure if he had tried to throw up in it or was hugging it in his sleep, but it was a strange look. Thankfully I wasn't met with anything unsightly in the toilet bowl, but there was a small crack in it now. Had he tried to get up by grabbing it? Wouldn't the hotel put a huge charge on his bill? At least paying for a toilet would hardly put a dent in his finances. I managed to get his wet lettuce of a body on its feet and saw his face was covered in sweat or tears. Had he cried himself to sleep here in the bathroom? On the floor was his phone, its screen smashed but still revealing a chat with someone named Lu. A name that could be male or female. I skimmed the conversation, which was in a mixture of English and Chinese. I wasn't absolutely sure, but it seemed like someone in his family had cancer and he needed to come back home as quickly as possible. Judging from the words and names, it looked like a Hong Kongese wife or husband. In any case, he clearly had a partner.

Despite my bad back, I managed to hoist up Habibi, who wasn't exactly petite, and lay him on the bed. It felt strange to see him spread out where I had lain only moments before. I stripped him of his suit. Hugo Boss shirt, Burberry trunks, Missoni socks, my God. Such was the taste of a forty-something Ivy Leaguer, and the cliché of it all was enough to drain my spirit.

Why had he called me here?

◊

When I got up the morning after that strange night, I saw that Habibi had left a note on the nightstand. He was going to a conference and would be back at the hotel late at night. On the table was a plate of room service leftovers and five 1,000-baht bills. Since it seemed a little excessive to be a maid's tip, I supposed he meant it for me. I pocketed it and ate one of the leftover chicken legs that were so skinny that I wondered if the chicken had been on a diet. It had gone cold and didn't taste great. The receipt next to the plate said it was about 20,000 Korean won. Judging from the price of things in Bangkok and the mass of the chicken, it was a pricey bird. I sat on the sofa and rubbed my legs. What was up with my circulation? I wasn't an old man yet.

In the afternoon, I went up to the outdoor pool on the tenth floor and swam in the sunlight. A straight white couple was nearby, splashing each other like crazy. There was one of those ubiquitous trios of Chinese people lying on the sunbeds. When I walked by, I heard one of them whisper in Mandarin, "Fat Korean." They thought I wouldn't understand. I tried hard not to laugh.

Who knew that even my almost nonexistent Mandarin would turn out to be useful? I sank underwater and studied the skinny legs of the white people.

I finished swimming and showered off, then went down to the Central Embassy shopping mall, hungry from the exercise.

On the second floor next to the Prada shop was a bakery called Paul, which I'd never heard of, and I made an impulse decision to eat there. I looked at the menu—filled with French and Thai words—and picked a pastry laden with olives and jalapeños as well as a latte. The bread was spicier than I expected and stung my nose. To think of all the idiots who bragged about how spicy Korean food was. I blew my nose in a napkin and messaged Habibi.

I took a swim and I'm having lunch. How is work? From your nuclear weapon.

He answered back that the conference was dragging on longer than he expected and he'd been invited to a dinner at the British Embassy and would come back to the hotel late. And that he was very sorry.

Don't be sorry. It was good news for me. Thinking over my reply, I wrote, *It's fine . . . No worries . . .* pretending to be more regretful than I really was with my plentiful ellipses. Sipping my latte, I launched Tinder and started swiping. This one went to Chulalongkorn University, that one to Thammasat, this one studied design, this one was Chinese, was biracial, was twenty-seven, was forty . . . Matches with strangers began to pile up. I was swiping through the men around me, wishing all these matches were money, when everything suddenly felt impossibly tedious and I put down my phone.

What if I went on a crazy shopping spree? Maxed out my card?

I left the bakery and looked around the other floors of the mall. Nike and Yves St. Laurent and Coffee Bean and Vivienne Westwood and Zara and Roberto Cavalli and Versace—I visited all of them but couldn't find anything I wanted. I took the escalator up to the other stores, but nothing struck my fancy. And by the time I got to one of the higher floors, thumping my fists on my tired thighs, I saw a familiar sign.

◊

This time last year, I'd gone into the same contact lens store that specialized in colored lenses. The night before, we had been dancing at a club, and Gyu-ho—in a fit of sheer enthusiasm—had thrown his head back and lost a lens. Gyu-ho's eyesight was so bad that the shop said they had only one product available that would work for him, and it happened to be one of those pupil-enlarging disposables. Gyu-ho said he'd rather wear the uncomfortable lenses instead of his Pororo glasses that shrank his eyes to the size of mustard seeds. We were offered a 15 percent discount if we paid in cash, but I didn't have enough baht in my wallet. I did have some won, however, and in the process of googling for a nearby currency exchange, we found a jewelry store a few doors down that converted currencies. I was on my way back to the lens store when a nylon jacket on a Zara mannequin seduced me into entering the store and buying it. By the time I got back to Gyu-ho, he was sitting at the lens shop with his normally sleepy-looking eyes so wide in the pupils that he looked like a drug addict or a rabbit detective in a Japanese anime. Blinking his sparkling eyes, Gyu-ho immediately began to admonish me.

—What took you so long? If I died waiting for you, would you be happy?

—Sorry. The sight of you is just too funny for words. Hello, Usami.

—Kumakichi! What is this you've bought?

I unfurled the jacket from the shopping bag and Gyu-ho sighed. Luckily the lenses could be paid for with the money I'd just exchanged. Gyu-ho put the lens box in the fanny pack he always wore (whether in Korea or Thailand). Stepping out of Central Embassy with Gyu-ho and his twice-dilated eyes, we looked around for the pharmacy he had researched beforehand and pinned on Google Maps. It was only twenty minutes away from the hotel on the BTS monorail.

Once we got off at the station near the pharmacy, I took over navigating, as Gyu-ho was bad with directions. My expectation had been that the place would be hidden away in some seedy alley, but it was right there on the main street. The interior was also the same as any other pharmacy. I showed the pharmacist a picture of the generic version of what I needed. The pharmacist, if he really was a pharmacist, took out a bottle of pills and explained to us, in English, how they worked. He said that taking just one a day at a set time was enough to perfectly prevent the disease. He really said the word "perfectly." How could he be so confident? He added that taking two of the pills before risky intercourse and then a pill every twenty-four hours for two more doses was enough to prevent transmission. I wrote all this down on the Notes app on my phone and wondered how different my life would be now if I'd had these pills seven years ago.

Would it have been very different? What would my life look like—better, worse, or the same as now? Thoughts led to more thoughts, but I abruptly got a hold of myself. We bought three bottles of the generics and a box of Kamagra liquid gels. It didn't even cost 200,000 won, but we were even offered a 10 percent discount on top of that if we paid in cash, so we did. Feeling like we'd spent too much money in one day, we got back to the hotel. We took out the vodka we'd gotten from duty-free, mixed it with calamansi juice bought from a convenience store, and drank it by the pool until the sun went down.

The next morning when we got up, we burst into laughter at the sight of each other's swollen faces. The result, likely, of drinking all night coupled with all those salty snacks. Gyu-ho, with his eyes half-closed, approached me with a pill and water. I popped one of these strange pills into Gyu-ho's mouth and one into mine.

—We're giving Kylie a vacation as well.

—Yeah.

After brushing our teeth side by side in front of the mirror, we showered together in the vast shower and quickly left the hotel. Quickly because we were afraid we'd end up napping again if we dawdled. No destination in mind, we began to walk where our feet took us.

—Where shall we go?

Gyu-ho said he wanted to see the ocean. I couldn't believe he had lived for twenty-odd years by the ocean and he still wanted to see more. *Aren't all oceans the same?* I thought, before I answered:

—The ocean is really far away from here.

—Why? It's Thailand. Isn't it surrounded by ocean?

—You're thinking of islands like Phuket or Koh Samui. This is Bangkok. It's like Seoul. We have to drive out for a while before we hit the ocean.

—So Bangkok is up on land as well.

Gyu-ho truly was the first person I'd ever met who used the phrase "up on land."

I remembered the time we had first met, how he'd answered my question about why he had come to Seoul: *It was my dream to come up on land.*

"On land," "my dream" . . . he sounded as sentimental as an old man from the postwar generation or a North Korean defector, enough to render me speechless for a moment—and I couldn't help bursting out laughing.

—Why're you laughing?

—Because you sound funny! Your accent is back.

—Stop laughing.

—Sorry. So what's your dream now?

—My dream . . . Hmm. Making lots of money. And . . .

—And what?

—Walking down the street at dawn with you, like this.

—Ugh . . .

I had scratched at my arm to hide my embarrassment, and snuck it around his. Something I never would've done normally, but he did say it was his dream, and who was I to deny him that? Even the hazy smog at the crossroads near Ewha's main gate at dawn made the setting ache with longing. Feeling like we were the only survivors left in a dystopia, we walked home together. I had drunk too fast and felt the alcohol dissipating from my brain with every step, but that was all right because I was with Gyu-ho.

Because soon we'd go to my shabby room and I'd pee toxic-smelling piss into a toilet with a weak flush, and we'd take our clothes off, shower, and lie down skin to skin in front of a whirling fan. Because it'd be just us left.

I couldn't believe it had been two years since we became a couple. It made me feel a flash of nostalgia, which made me reach out and brush the skin on Gyu-ho's elbow. That was the extent of the public display of affection Gyu-ho had allowed me in Thailand, the heat being his excuse. He looked over at me, eyes sparkling, and asked:

—What shall we do now?

—Do you want to see the river instead of the ocean? They've got a big river here, like the Han. The Chao Phraya, just twenty minutes by taxi. We can take a boat from there to Khao San Road.

—Yeah. I've heard of it. Khao San Road. Let's go there.

We jumped into a taxi to go to a pier and hopped onto a long boat that arrived spewing black smoke, a ferry that would take us down the river for the affordable price of around 700 won. The ferries must have been an important commuting service, because we saw students in uniforms as well as office workers crowd on with us. Feeling like we were on a cruise, we squeezed into two of the tiny plastic orange seats, our shoulders smashed against each other. The boat shook more than I expected as it started to move, and it pitched forward with a groaning sound. We were only five minutes into our cruise up the river when rain clouds suddenly darkened the sky.

—It's going to rain? You said it was the dry season.

—I said it was the late rainy season.

—Isn't that the dry season?

—I guess even the late rainy season is still the rainy season.

—Hey, look over there.

The rain-heavy clouds were approaching swiftly enough for their motion to be perceived with the naked eye, and we were suddenly inside the rain with wind lashing right into the open sides of the boat. The other passengers, apparently used to the situation, got up and unfurled the tarps at the edges of the roof above us. Following their lead, we also rolled down the tarp. And as soon as they were all down, a real deluge began. We could hear the valiant sound of the engine, but the boat refused to move forward. Lightning flashed and thunder rolled, and thick strands of rain beat atop the roof of the boat. Rainwater seeped through the edges of the tarp, and it fogged over. We gripped each other's knees and endured the rocking. The feeling of Gyu-ho's hot knee in my hand made me feel strangely sleepy. The tossing of the boat didn't make me anxious at all. I had my hand on his knee until my palm was wet with sweat. Saying his knee was hot, Gyu-ho removed my hand and placed it in his own icy palm. We stopped at two or three more piers, where the passengers crowding the boat almost all disembarked. The rain was still just as strong even by the time our sweaty palms moved onto the cold handrails. We had been planning to get off at the next pier and catch a taxi as soon as the rain let up, but the downpour refused to cease. And the emptier the boat, the rockier the ride became. Gyu-ho said he was feeling nauseous.

We finally decided to get off the boat at the next pier.

—We're up on land, Gyu-ho, just like you've always dreamed of.

—God, I thought I was going to die of seasickness.

We couldn't wait out the storm underneath an awning at the pier. This was no brief rain but a full-on downpour. There were no shops anywhere that we could see, not even people.

—Oh, Gyu-ho, what are we going to do?

Gyu-ho took my phone and put it along with his own phone inside the red fanny pack he had slung over his shoulder. Then he grabbed my hand. We dashed into the rainy streets. In less than thirty seconds, our clothes were drenched. We wanted to get an umbrella at a convenience store, but there wasn't so much as a 7-Eleven anywhere. I was running out of breath, my feet were hurting, and I wondered what the point of running was anymore. I begged Gyu-ho to stop, said we should walk, but maybe he didn't hear me because he kept pulling me along. I couldn't stand it any longer—I barked at him to go slower. Gyu-ho turned his surprised-rabbit eyes back toward me. I wanted to smile back, but my face kept crumpling. There was a brief silence between us. Gyu-ho suddenly lay down flat on the pavement.

—What are you doing?

—What do you mean, what am I doing? I'm tired. I'm lying down.

—But why lie down in the middle of the street?

—I used to do this often as a kid, in Seogwipo.

—You used to lie in the street?

—Yeah, I loved lying down flat on the road next to the beach. That was my thing.

—That's really dangerous. I'm amazed you made it off the island alive. Why would you do that?

—I just liked it. It cooled me down. It was comfortable. I could see the sky, and it felt like it was covering me like a blanket.

—What is this, you're reciting poetry? Come on, get up.

When I reached for his hand, he grabbed it and pulled me down. I teetered and fell into a sitting position.

—Lie down with me.

Jesus, was he nuts? But when I saw his face—Gyu-ho, who always seemed more at peace than anyone else I knew—my heart melted a little. Well, I was already drenched, after all. So I lay down next to him on the road. The rain kept hitting my eyes, making me squint up at the sky. A sky with a thousand wriggles, like someone had dumped water on a huge piece of paper. Like Gyu-ho and I had covered ourselves with a dirty blanket. He closed his eyes and said:

—I really like this.

—We're soaked to our underwear, what's there to like?

—Just you and me being here together. That's what I like.

3.

Habibi returned late that night. When I opened the door for him, I saw he had a shopping bag in one hand. His usually gray face was a little flushed—he must've done some drinking at his evening function. I'd only spent two days with him, but he was beginning to feel like family. Maybe because he actually was a family man, someone used to putting down roots and flowering. The shopping bag contained macarons printed with the Mandarin Oriental Shop logo. Habibi said that I seemed to have enjoyed them and so he bought them for me. Having followed Gyu-ho to all sorts of shops in search of sweet things, I had inadvertently become addicted to sugar myself. Habibi slipped a pink macaron into my mouth. I chewed about half of it and left the rest on the nightstand. When I was with Habibi, I sometimes felt like I was a child, and sometimes a parent. As he took off his trousers, Habibi told me about his day (as if I were interested). The big house in front of the hotel was not a private residence but the British Embassy. They had set up tables in its beautiful English garden, and he had eaten steak, lobster, and scallops with ravioli with the British and Thai bureaucrats. There were to be fireworks in celebration of the peace and prosperity between the two nations, which is why he had rented a room where we could see them. Habibi, in his trunks, went up to the window and pointed to some faraway spot.

—Tonight, we are going to see the most beautiful fireworks in the world.

Fireworks are fireworks, what the hell does he mean by "the most beautiful"? Probably the most expensive. So fucking what?

—It'll be so loud you won't be able to sleep. They're going to set off firecrackers on the street by the embassy.

Everything suddenly seemed unbearable. I went into the bathroom without answering him and began to draw a bath. Even before the tub filled up, I plunged my head into the water. All I could see down there were the shadows rippling on the surface. Everything was calm, the only sound being the water hitting the surface. I liked that. I wished the whole universe would stop turning and pause, just in that moment.

I held my breath for as long as I could, then lifted my head.

You must've been a fish in a past life.

Gyu-ho said that to me once because I would take a bath in every motel we went to that had a tub.

You do realize that someone has probably pissed and shit in there at some point.

When I suggested he join me, Gyu-ho would refuse, like I'd offered him a soak in a sewer. Unfazed, I would fill the tub to the brim and submerge completely to the top of my head. Submerging my head brought my knees out, and made me want to buy a tub as big as a swimming pool when I made a lot of money someday.

I dumped an entire mini bottle of that Le Labo body cleanser from the amenity tray into the water jet, which immediately made mountains of foam leap up like whipped cream. I closed my eyes, wishing I could suffocate in the foam.

◊

That day, we eventually ended up at an unfamiliar guesthouse.

In Bangkok, taxis would magically stop in front of us when we so much as raised an arm, just like in television dramas, but not that day. It rained so heavily that the water came up to our ankles, and I couldn't see any taxis on the road. We held hands and walked through the mazelike alleys of private residences, looking for a place we could sit down to rest for a bit. That's how we came upon a sign that said: GUESTHOUSE. We entered right away.

It was about 50,000 won for a room with no bathroom and a ceiling fan instead of air-conditioning. Considering Bangkok prices and the shabby state of the building, we were clearly being ripped off, but we were in no position to haggle. We burst out laughing when we saw the room—its only piece of furniture was a single mattress that almost completely filled up the space, making it more of a coffin than a room. Gyu-ho and I took turns in the communal shower (a euphemism for what was actually just a separate space down the hall with a showerhead and drain), where we washed ourselves with lukewarm water, then spread the bath towels the front desk had given us over the mattress and lay down next to each other. The large steel ceiling fan spun overhead with a tapping sound, and I made a stupid comment—"If that thing falls on us, we're mincemeat"—to which Gyu-ho obligingly replied, "Let's be hamburger patties together forever," as he stretched his arm toward me. His shorter-than-average arm wasn't a good fit for my larger-than-average head, but we pretended to be comfortable as we lay still like that. I have no idea who started kissing whom first. Our damp bodies came together and Gyu-ho got on top of me.

—Do you have it?

The only "it" we had in Gyu-ho's fanny pack on the floor were two packets of lube, crumpled from age. We must've used up the condoms.

—What do we do . . . ? Do you think it's OK?

Looking at Gyu-ho's worried face, I ripped open the lube packet with my teeth.

We had sex. For the first time in the two years we had been a couple, we had unprotected sex.

I gazed at Gyu-ho crushing my body, feeling his mass. His heat, his breath, the gaze of his large, black pupils. What was once a part of him flowed into me and became me.

After we had sex, I closed my eyes to rest for a moment. But when I opened them again, it was already dim around us. It was impossible to tell if it was night or day, but the rain had finally ceased. Gyu-ho's face was near mine. He was asleep. I stared at him for a long time. I wiped the droplets of sweat on his nose, gazed up at the whirling ceiling fan above, and wished the universe would pause in that moment.

◊

I still sometimes think that if I just reach out, I could touch the bridge of his nose.

That was only an illusion. The reality before me was my swollen, wrinkled hand. Gaining weight made my fingers and even fingertips ugly. I had to get rid of the habit of falling asleep wherever I was. It was after four o'clock by the time I got out of the bath. Habibi had dozed off. When had he fallen asleep? Had he been drunk enough to leave me in the bath? He might've been awake for the fireworks, but I had a feeling he hadn't been. I gently swept his hair from his sleeping face. Hair flecked with gray. Wrinkles that were deeper beneath the light of the lamp.

Why had he brought me here? Had he simply wanted someone to be waiting for him when he came back to the room? For someone to turn the lights on, to mess up the room a bit, to speak into the silence even in an unfamiliar language? Because he traveled so much for business. Because he knew the coldness of a pillow he'd lain on once before, or the texture of starched sheets, sharp enough to wound. Or because of all these things. Then why was I here with him? I looked down at the shattered screen of his phone on the floor.

There was no way of knowing whether there'd been fireworks or not. Everything seemed to have passed by in the blink of an eye. At some point, my life had turned into one dimly remembered night after another.

I lowered the lights slightly and left the room. Once I closed the door behind me, strangely enough, I ceased to remember Habibi's face.

◊

On the first day of the year, Gyu-ho and I went on a trip to Wolmido Island. We ate hot dogs wrapped in thick, fried dough, and braved a Viking-themed ride on which the safety bar wobbled as if it would give way any minute. In our competition to outscream each other, my voice went hoarse in ten seconds. Right next to the theme park was a coin-op noraebang, where we sang breakup ballads that went up to pitches we couldn't reach, as well as the usual joyous dance-idol songs. After about ten songs, it was time for the sunrise. Hoping to catch it, we walked to the beach. Despite my padded jacket, I was cold, and I slipped my hands into his armpits.

—What's the meaning of this, Kumakichi!

I laughed and hugged him from behind. Intertwined, we waddled toward the sand. People were gathered at the shore. As the merciless winds whipped across my face, I wondered if Gyu-ho's childhood winters by the sea were like this.

There was a crowd near the giant tetrapod breakwaters, which we approached. A woman with red lipstick, an upswept hairdo, and a gentle smile was passing out lanterns and markers to the people gathered. She handed us lanterns and markers as well, and said that if we wrote a wish inside, she would light the lantern for us to send it floating into the sky. Gyu-ho whispered:

—She must be Chinese.

I nodded, and the lady said:

—In China, we have a tradition where we write our wishes inside a lantern and send it up into the sky on the first day of the year.

We spread out the lantern on the ground and wrote our wishes. Gyu-ho seemed to be sure of what he was wishing for. Eternal love between Kumakichi and Usami, winning the lottery, conquering the universe . . . I thought about what to write at first but like Gyu-ho ended up writing whatever came to mind.

We finished up and handed over the lantern to the lady. She deftly handled the wires at the bottom to set it up with a tea light. I gave her a tiny wrapped chocolate that I'd had in my pocket for who knows how long, and she smiled at me like someone who had never known sadness in her life. A group of lanterns went up at the same time. We cheered as we gazed at the lanterns floating gently up into the sky. Everyone with their happy faces. As if our wishes had already been granted.

◊

As I left the hotel, I began walking wherever my feet took me. The sun wasn't up, but there were already pedestrians in business suits on their way to work. I would've looked the same whenever I had a writing deadline. Wearing a suit and sitting in a café near my office at dawn, crouched over the table and furiously composing or editing something.

It must've rained overnight, because the air smelled of dust. After about ten minutes of walking, I went into a convenience store. I wasn't hungry but wanted to buy something and ended up with seaweed snacks that had Korean idols on the packaging and a two-for-one deal on strawberry milk. Plastic bag in hand, I continued my walk on this aimless journey. Past a wall was a narrow path just wide enough for one person to pass. Right inside the alley was the hole to a sewer with rats running around below. I tried to walk without looking down until I came to some sliding doors. They were metal and had windows like the kind I used to see on old rice cake shops or general stores. When I walked inside, I realized that I was not inside a shop but in a small courtyard with houses on both sides, their sliding doors wide open without even a screen against mosquitoes, the inhabitants and their lives completely visible. I worried about the bugs they must get inside. Suddenly curious, and despite knowing this was very rude, I peered inside the houses. The people seemed too busy to take notice of me. A man washed his face in front of a basin, a woman next to him rinsed some vegetables, an old man sat on the floor and shucked corn, and another woman sat in front of her dressing table and frantically toweled her hair. At the end of the courtyard was a house with an old mattress in the middle of it. Two children, around four or five years old, were jumping up and down on it. Every squeak of the spring made a nearby cat with milky film over its eyes flinch. *Think of the dust*. My feet stopped of their own accord. Even though they couldn't possibly reach it, the children stretched their hands out to the ceiling, trying to tap it with every jump. I remembered what Gyu-ho said to me once.

—I want to ride a bang-bang.

—You mean a bong-bong pogo stick?

—They called them bong-bongs in your neighborhood?

—Yeah, they call them bang-bangs in Jeju?

—I don't know about the whole island, but it was bang-bang where I lived.

—You used to see them everywhere.

Before I knew it, I was sitting on the edge of a stranger's porch. The cat ran away. Noticing me, the children stopped their jumping. The slightly smaller child hid behind the bigger one. I took out the two bottles of strawberry milk from the plastic bag. I opened and sipped from one, then offered the other bottle to the kids. They didn't approach me. Smiling, I put it down on the porch. As if watching the most fascinating sight in the world, the children watched me drink my milk. When I finished it, I asked the children if they'd seen the fireworks the other night. They didn't seem to understand. I asked where their parents were, and there was similarly no answer.

—Where have they gone, leaving you all by yourselves?

I'd mumbled the words under my breath, but they suddenly made my nose smart from rising tears, which, surely, was some weird sign of growing old. I looked up at the sky to knock the threatening tears back. Droplets of water on the awning were about to fall. It must've rained in the night. Had the fireworks been canceled because of it?

Rain still falls during the late rainy season, as do tears even when it's too late.

◊

After breaking up with Gyu-ho, I kept having nightmares.

In my dreams, he and I are laughing and talking it up, and he tells me he loves me. But even in my dream, I know it isn't Gyu-ho. The moment I go up to him and hear his breathing and hug his shoulders, he disappears. He scatters like sand or turns into dark liquid like sewage and flows away. I've no choice but to stand at arm's length. Watching him, listening to his voice, wishing this time would last forever.

Waking up from such dreams, I'm drenched in sweat.

Lately I've felt like I'm crumbling away little by little. Like Gyu-ho in my memories, I am breaking down and scattering into ashes. The feeling is so clear to me that it's hard to shake it off like I usually would.

Sometimes his very existence to me is the existence of love itself.

I think that for a while now, using the medium of writing, I've tried to prove over and over again in many other stories I've written that the relationship between Gyu-ho and me was something so special to us that no one could take it away from us, that it was 100 percent real. Using all kinds of other methods to create Gyu-ho and write him as other characters, I've tried to show the relationship we had and the time we spent together as complete as they were, but the more I try, the further I get from him and the emotions I had back then. My efforts become something fainter and more distanced from the truth. The made-up Gyu-ho in my writing got hurt or died many times, and is always resurrected, as if love saves his life—whereas the real Gyu-ho lives and breathes and keeps moving on. The greater the gap between the two becomes, the harder it gets to endure it. I've tried and tried for a long time, but it's only made me realize more clearly than ever that all I have left is a handful of empty words scattering away and leaving me behind as I sit here, scribbling. My shoulders hunched forward, a deep frown on my face, the world so small that I can hear my own breathing.

◊

The lantern we sent up that day did not go far. The moment it made it past the breakwaters, it caught fire and spewed black smoke over the water before crashing into some faraway waves. Some of the people around us started laughing. Smiling, the woman in the red lipstick commented that there must've been a hole somewhere in the paper. I looked back and forth between the other lanterns that were flying far away and the spot that ours had fallen into. I stared at it for a long time. The other people started to move on, going their own way. Gyu-ho also turned and walked away, but I couldn't get myself to leave. It was unbelievable to me that my wish had fizzled.

I'd started writing so many things on that lantern, fixing my life many times. To succeed in my diet, to win the apartment lottery, to have a Porsche Cayenne, to have a bestselling debut . . . None of them was what I really wished for, so I crossed all the words out. That was how the lantern ended up with a hole, I bet.

In the end, I left just two syllables on the lantern.

Gyu-ho.

My only wish.

Acknowledgments

Already, my second published book.

I didn't know this while I was first writing the work that would become *Love in the Big City*, but the process of putting my stories together and revising them to write this novel was one that made me feel embarrassed for myself again and again. So much of this book leans on the past, both on my own personal history and that of many people around me.

As I kept thinking through my past, wanting to live as someone who was myself and myself alone, it was hard to accept that I was, indeed, the person that I was when I first wrote the words in this book. These contradictory feelings created a difficult situation for both me and the people around me. To have written a book about them with a title as fancy as *Love in the Big City* seems, I don't know, a little less than conscientious . . . but what can I do. To all the people who bought me drinks and willingly gave me a part of their lives as well as their precious emotions (I was admittedly not the greatest person to receive them), I only want to say how sincerely grateful I am for such gifts, and for how we tried our best, even if we are no longer together.

There have been many changes during the year I spent editing this book. The Constitutional Court declared the statute criminalizing abortion to be unconstitutional, rendering the "crime" of abortion obsolete. HIV PrEP was approved by Korea's authorities and our national health insurance began covering it for high-risk demographics. All writers are condemned to depict their worlds at least a step or two behind, which can be overwhelming, but for at least this citizen-writer, the fact that society changes faster than my writing can catch up is a joyful thing.

"Young," who narrates the four stories in this book, is simultaneously the same person and different people. The person who is writing this now is perhaps someone very different from who I really am, a person who could be someone you know very well, even yourself, the one person you wanted to avoid at all costs because you're feeling too overwhelmed. Way before I became a writer, I was just a young person in the Noughties trying to make it from day to day, and also a citizen of the Republic of Korea, and writing and speaking of the issues I write and speak about was a desperate act for me.

I was desperate enough to pour everything I had into this act.

As I tackled these sensitive issues head-on, I tried hard not to forget that I was also not free from these issues nor completely guiltless myself. It required a considerable amount of courage.

Last year, when my first book came out in Korea, I began receiving feedback from readers for the first time. There were good comments and bad comments, and some that were hard to endure, but there was one particular kind of comment that remains in my memory.

"Thank you for writing about us, about me."

These were the words from readers sharing that they were queer or stuck in difficult situations. In real life, I am a fearful and highly anxious person, but it was their sincere words, words that they had put together with great effort and courage in order to share them with me, that made this book possible. I hope that I have now somehow passed over that effortfulness and courage to you, the person who is now bent over this book somewhere, reading these words.

When I write—or when I'm going about my day—I sometimes feel as vague and uncertain as if I'm all alone wandering through a cloud of dust, but sometimes I feel a warmth, like my hands have touched something. I want to call that something love. I know all too well how this emotion called love, how the word itself, can easily crumble into nothing, but all I can do is tightly grip this tiny bit of warmth and embrace it with all my might. Just so I can live on as myself. Just so I can live this life as myself and myself alone.

Summer 2019
From Seoul, the big city that I love,
Sang Young Park

* The engineering student's text message in "Jaehee" is a line taken from *2da's Uncut and Unlimited Play* (Random House Korea, 2008).

* The HIV PrEP (pre-exposure prophylaxis) scene in "Late Rainy Season Vacation" was written using information from "Truvada for PrEP Fact Sheet: Ensuring Safe and Proper Use" (FDA, 2012) and "Pre-exposure Prophylaxis (PrEP) for HIV Prevention" (CDC, 2014). It is also said to have been proven that the same pill taken within seventy-two hours of "high-risk sexual behavior" followed by a daily twenty-eight-day regimen is effective in preventing HIV infection (consultant: Kim Wu-yong, preventive medicine specialist).

* While the geographic locations of this work are based in fact, all characters and incidents are fiction.